SEARCH AND RESCUE

―――――― PENTAGON ESCAPE

SEARCH AND RESCUE

PENTAGON ESCAPE

ALEX LONDON

SCHOLASTIC INC.

All rights reserved. Published by Scholastic Inc., *Publishers since 1920.* SCHOLASTIC and associated logos are trademarks and/or registered trademarks of Scholastic Inc.

The publisher does not have any control over and does not assume any responsibility for author or third-party websites or their content.

This book is a work of fiction. Names, characters, places, and incidents are either the product of the author's imagination or are used fictitiously, and any resemblance to actual persons, living or dead, business establishments, events, or locales is entirely coincidental.

ISBN 978-1-338-89318-2

10 9 8 7 6 5 4 3 2 1   23 24 25 26 27

First edition, September 2023

Printed in the U.S.A. 40

Book design by Maithili Joshi

To the helpers

MIKEY: 8:15 A.M.

My visitor's badge is red and shiny and says they can shoot me if they want to.

Okay, technically it says that if I wander off without my escort or am found in a restricted area of the Pentagon, they can arrest me. But when you're wearing what is basically a bright red poster on a chain around your neck that tells everyone where you aren't supposed to be, you don't think too deeply about the details. You think about the guys with guns guarding this place.

It's weird that my dad works here. He's such a nerd.

It's even weirder that he's bringing me to work today.

And it's the weirdest thing of all that his employer—the United States Department of Defense—is saying that if I leave my dad's side without permission, they can arrest me.

I never thought the government would get involved

in my dad's parenting, but I guess they have been for a while, since the court gave him sole custody of me. It's for the best, I know, and my dad's a good guy, but he's not exactly Mr. Warm-and-Fuzzy, and he's not as fun as Mom. He is responsible though. He never lets me go to school without lunch money or my homework. And he is not in jail, which gives him another advantage over Mom.

Yeah, I've got that kind of sad story, but it's not all bad.

Like, aside from the threat of lethal force, it's pretty cool that I get to come in to my dad's office today. He's a civilian contractor at the Pentagon, the United States military's headquarters, which means he's not *in* the military, but he's employed *by* the military and works alongside the sailors, soldiers, airmen, and Marines who also work in the Pentagon. Also accountants. There are a lot of accountants.

Within the military, he works for the Defense Intelligence Agency, which is, like, top-secret nerd stuff. Which, again, makes sense because my dad is 100 percent a nerd. His favorite joke: "You know how I keep track of all the terrible Dad jokes I tell? In a *Dada-base!*"

I've heard that a hundred times and I groan every single time.

At work, however, he doesn't tell bad Dad jokes. His boss is a general, with stars on his uniform and everything. Only one star, but that's enough stars for everyone he meets in the halls to call him sir.

When we get to my dad's department inside the DIA's offices on the first floor of the Pentagon, there's a big buzz-cut guy in a Marine Corps uniform waiting outside his cubicle for a meeting. My dad shakes his hand and I give the guy a salute.

"Morning, sir," I tell him.

"Don't call me sir, son." He points to the three chevron insignia on his sleeve. "I work for a living."

"Sorry," I mumble, and he laughs and shakes my hand.

"Sergeant Guinsler," he introduces himself, then looks to my dad. "I miss a Bring Your Kid to Work Day memo?"

"No, Sergeant," my dad tells him. "Mikey here has to do a report for school on an American landmark, and his teacher gave him permission to come in today for research."

"Landmark, huh?" Sergeant Guinsler says. "You

3

know, I was assigned to the Pentagon early on in my career to give tours to VIPs. I'd be happy to show your son around real quick if you want to get settled before our meeting?"

My dad looks relieved. He works in this huge building but knows next to nothing about it. He's a computer guy and spends most of his time staring at a screen and testing lines of code for bugs. I know it's important work, because everyone says the 2000s are gonna be the era when "the battlefield goes digital," but it seems pretty dull to me. Also, the US isn't at war, so, like, what battlefield?

He works on something called Secure Communications Development Operations, which he sometimes calls SCDO, but most of the time he calls it *skidoo*, like the snowmobile I rode on vacation one time.

The snowmobile was way more fun than my dad's job is. He once tried to tell me about network security protocols and I nearly died of boredom. I wonder if that's what he's really working on here, a weapon that can kill the enemy through intense and sustained boredom.

I'm really excited by the idea someone else will give me this tour of the Pentagon. I bet Sergeant Guinsler has way better stories.

4

"Thank you," my dad tells him. Sergeant Guinsler laughs.

"I should thank you," he says. "This gets me out of the morning Program and Budget meeting. This guy right here is my personal hero." He claps my dad on the shoulder and we all laugh, though I'm not sure what's so funny.

The closest my dad ever got to doing something actually heroic was last year, when he had to debug a thousand computers for Y2K, which I didn't really understand, but it had everyone freaked out that if the computers didn't get fixed the world was gonna, like, end. My dad did something to make sure that nuclear submarine commanders could still talk to the commanders in this building if they needed to, without accidentally starting World War Three. World War Three didn't start, so I guess he did his job well.

Now he does something that he says he's not even allowed to talk about, but it still looks the same to me. A glowing screen, fingers tapping on keys, and a lot of coffee. A young man in uniform sits at another desk tapping keys on his computer and then waves toward my dad, calling him over.

He checks the clock on the wall. Eight fifteen. He

turns to Sergeant Guinsler. "We're not till nine, right?"

"Right," confirms Sergeant Guinsler. "I'll get Mikey back in time."

My dad goes to talk to the young man, who has some question about whatever he's studying on his screen. It's funny that this guy and Sergeant Guinsler are both in the military, because he's a skinny geek in glasses, who's probably spent more time playing first-person shooter games than actually shooting a gun. Sergeant Guinsler doesn't look like he's ever played a video game in his life, but he has probably shot a lot of guns. Then again, he works in this computer-nerd office, so maybe looks can be deceiving.

"What do you say, Mikey?" he asks me. "Wanna get the real story of this place?"

"I'd love that, sir . . . I mean, er, Sarge." I grin and he grins back. I can't help but like the guy.

He notices me picking at the tight tie knotted around my neck. I'm dressed up for the office visit. "You wanna lose the necklace?" he jokes, and I nod eagerly. My dad thought it'd be good for me to wear a tie, but I feel like it's choking me. I yank it off and Sergeant Guinsler puts out his hand for it. Then he whistles.

"Hey, Dave!" My dad turns. "Heads up!" He tosses the balled-up tie to my dad, who looks puzzled but sticks it in his pocket. "Now we're ready, yes?" Sergeant Guinsler smiles.

"Yes, Sergeant!" I say in my best pretend boot camp voice, which makes him chuckle. "Should we start back there?"

I point to the heavy doors that lead to the secure room, called a SCIF, which stands for Sensitive Compartmented Information Facility. The military loves acronyms. It feels like they have acronyms for everything: SCIF. SCDO. Even MRE, which stands for Meal, Ready to Eat, and is the food that soldiers often have to eat in the field. It's freeze-dried and vacuum sealed and famously gross. Sergeant Guinsler makes a face like I'd just offered him one.

"Sorry, kiddo," he says. "Can't take you in there. You don't have clearance. An alarm will go off if you even cross that threshold."

"How?"

"There's an RFID chip in your visitor's badge," he says. "Radio-frequency identification."

Since my dad's office does top-secret work, I guess it makes sense that I'm not allowed in the secure room, just in the rows and rows and rows of cubicles outside. It kind of reminds me of those mazes they use to do experiments on mice. Except the cubicles are all in neat rows with aisles between them, so it'd be just about the easiest maze in the world to solve, even for a mouse.

The Pentagon itself, however, is like a giant mouse maze.

My dad's office is 1C535, which means it's on the first floor of what they call C-Ring, near Corridor Five, so that's where Sergeant Guinsler starts my tour, in the hallways outside my dad's office.

SCDO is a small part of the Defense Intelligence Agency, which is a massive network of spies and soldiers and civilians all over the world. The offices at the Pentagon are just a tiny part of the agency, and no one person really knows everything they do. Most of this office is for budgeting and personnel and planning stuff. Not, like, James Bond–type action. Just because they're a super-top-secret organization inside an already top-secret organization doesn't mean what they do is exciting. Mostly it looks like they write reports, share reports, and have meetings about those reports. All that reporting keeps them pretty busy. No one pays me or Sergeant Guinsler much attention at all.

All over the place, people hustle this way and that, doing everything from planning wars to planning lunches. There are entire departments that do nothing but organize travel for other departments that do nothing but organize seminars about the work still other departments do deciding what equipment to buy for still more departments in the massive military machine. Most of what the thousands of people who work here every day do is pretty dull, in fact.

"Upward of twenty thousand people work in the Pentagon," Sergeant Guinsler tells me in his tour guide voice. "Although today, there are fewer people because of a construction and modernization project. You'll notice the scaffolding in the hall between Corridors Four and Five. They're upgrading a lot in this old place. You picked an auspicious day to be here. You know what *auspicious* means?"

"I'm in seventh grade," I tell him.

"That's not what I asked," he replies.

"I didn't think I'd be getting a vocabulary quiz today, Sergeant," I answer. "But *auspicious* means 'favorable or suggesting good luck.'"

"Very good. Do you know *why* today is an auspicious day?"

MIKEY: 8:45 A.M.

Our tour starts in the center courtyard of the Pentagon, outside A-Ring. It's a five-acre courtyard with landscaping and benches and places where the workers can get fresh air, take walks, even eat breakfast and lunch outside on nice days like today. Small groups of people are going this way and that, some in military uniforms, some in civilian clothes. I'm amazed by how many different sorts of people work here: It's like a picture of America itself. There's even a lady with a baby in her arms, trying to calm them from crying.

We watch for a minute as she soothes the baby, then rushes back inside through one of the big Corridor Four doors to go back to her office.

"Maybe it really *is* Bring Your Kid to Work Day," I joke.

Sergeant Guinsler doesn't laugh this time. He drops his voice to a whisper. "That's one of the mutant babies in the classified Government Mutant Program, Sub-basement Seven. Don't tell anyone you saw that."

Sergeant Guinsler delivers that line so straight, I can't tell if he's joking or not until he bursts out laughing. "Oh, your face! Nah, that's Lena Stanwick, a clerk in the Navy Command Center. She couldn't get a babysitter today."

I shake my head. "Are you gonna mess with me like that all morning?" I ask. "You know I'm doing this for school, right?"

"Hey, it's not my fault if you're gullible," the sergeant says. "Gum?"

He offers me a stick of cinnamon gum. I don't usually like cinnamon gum, but my dad always jokes that when someone offers you a stick of gum you should take it, because maybe they're trying to tell you your breath is bad.

I take the gum and he gives me the whole pack with a wink. I use my hand to try to smell my own breath, but you can't really do that, can you? I don't smell anything wrong with it. Sergeant Guinsler laughs a little.

"You're fine, Mikey," he said. "I just thought kids like gum."

"Um, yeah, thanks," I say, putting the pack into my pocket. "You don't have kids, do you?"

"Let's get started," he tells me, changing the subject

and turning his voice back to tour guide mode. "The Pentagon is built over twenty-nine acres, with another sixty-seven acres of parking lots. It's built in a true pentagon, with five sides and five concentric rings labeled A through E from the inside to the outside. Each is five stories high, connected by central corridors radiating out from this central courtyard where we're standing."

"Is it true that Moscow had two nuclear weapons aimed here throughout the Cold War?" I ask.

Sergeant Guinsler nods. "They thought this courtyard was a launch site for one of our nuclear missiles. They saw high-ranking officers go to that building in the center there at the same time every day and assumed it was a secure meeting spot." He points to a little building with a wooden owl on the top right at the center of the courtyard.

"So there is no nuclear weapon under here?" I confirm, taking notes in the little pad I'd brought. I'd heard this story too.

"What do you think?" he asks.

"I mean, officers go there at the same time every day?" I ask, thinking. "What time?"

"Around noon."

I grin. "It's a lunch spot," I announce.

"Correct!" Sergeant Guinsler claps. "That hot dog stand is known as Cafe Ground Zero, because the Soviets had no less than two nuclear weapons pointed at it at all times."

I look at the unassuming building in the middle of the large park. I look around at the workers coming and going between their offices.

"Is that true though?" I ask. "Didn't the Russians have spies all over this building? They would've known it was just a hot dog stand."

Sergeant Guinsler sighs. "You're too smart for your own good, Mikey. Never let logic get in the way of a good story."

"But it's not true."

"Fiction can tell some truths better than facts can."

"I think a good story should at least be logical," I reply.

"Life isn't logical," he responds. "Sometimes, stuff happens that logic can't explain. Miracles, surprises. When you're older, you'll understand. Logic only gets you so far in life. Sometimes, there's more value in the illogical."

"You don't talk like my dad and the other programmer guys he works with," I say.

"No, I don't," Sergeant Guinsler tells me. "I actually

meant to be a chaplain when I started my career. I got into intelligence work because of it. It's all about understanding people and listening to what they say, and what they don't say. And paying *attention*." He pauses, then pops another quiz question on me. "So, are you paying attention? Why do you think this building was built as a pentagon?"

I pause to think. "Well, the shape with all the corridors cutting through it means that everywhere is kind of connected to everywhere else," I say. "So if you wanted to get from one place to another, you wouldn't have to walk around the whole building. You could cut between the rings and across the courtyard to get around."

"Right again," said Sergeant Guinsler. "When it was built, the architects knew it was huge. Six million square feet of office space, which is three times the size of the Empire State Building. If it were built in the usual way, it'd be impossible to cross quickly. So they designed it with the idea that the longest walk anyone could take between offices was about ten minutes. There's even a drive between Rings B and C, so that vehicles can get around. And tunnels out from this courtyard to the North and the South Parking Lots."

"So it's meant to look imposing but is actually easy to navigate?" I ask.

"It's supposed to be," says Sergeant Guinsler, "but over the years, offices have been added and divided and rearranged, so it creates a kind of maze of blocked hallways and switchbacks around all the rings. I'll show you what I mean."

He leads me around to Corridor Four and we go back inside. Before we step in, I take one last look at the clear blue sky and the serene courtyard. It's so calm that it's hard to imagine there was a time this place had been targeted by deadly nuclear weapons. Weird to think that people just came and went to work during those days with the knowledge that they had targets on their backs. If the nukes did get launched, there'd be nothing they could do to save themselves.

I make a note in my pad to ask Sergeant Guinsler if there were bomb shelters here, and what they're used for now that the Cold War is over and the danger of nuclear annihilation has passed.

First though, he takes me to the brand-new Navy Command Center, which is one of the highest-tech offices in the building—at least that I'm allowed to see. It's sprawling, spreading between Rings D and C and taking up almost a third of an acre. It even has a huge open Watch Floor, staffed twenty-four hours a day like a mission control. The people there monitor Navy ships and aircraft all over the world in real time. Unlike my dad's nerdy cubicles, this looks like how I think a military headquarters *should* look.

Except that when we walk in, no one even looks at us. Everyone is watching TV monitors tuned to cable news and whispering to each other with worried looks on their faces.

We make our way over to Lena Stanwick, where she has her baby in a carrier next to her desk and is watching a small television in disbelief. On the screen, there's a giant fire and billowing smoke from one of the Twin Towers of the World Trade Center in New York City.

"What's up, Lena?" Sergeant Guinsler asks. The woman shakes her head, dismayed.

"It looks like a plane crashed into the World Trade Center," she says. "Some type of accident."

Sergeant Guinsler exhales slowly. "Awful," he says. "Someone messed up big-time."

"Those poor people," she mutters, switching the screen off and absently stroking her baby's tiny hand in their carrier. She finally looks up at us and sees me, which brings a smile to her face. "And who is this young man?"

"You know Dave from DIA?" Sergeant Guinsler asks. "This is his son, Mikey."

"Nice to meet you." I offer my hand, and Lena shakes it gently.

"He's doing a report for school on the Pentagon," the sergeant tells her. "You have any interesting facts you think he should know? Watch out though, he's a clever one. Saw right through the hot dog stand story."

"I don't know why every tour guide tells that story," she says. "But I'm glad *some* people have more sense than to believe it." She winks at me, and just then, her baby makes a little burbling sound.

"Can I meet your little one?" Sergeant Guinsler asks. Lena lifts her baby from their cozy spot and lets him hold them. The baby looks so tiny in the big Marine's massive arms, but Sergeant Guinsler is gentle. He cradles the baby against his huge biceps, cooing and making little kissy noises. I guess even some hard-core Marines turn into mush around cute babies.

"You wanna hold him?" Lena asks me. I just shake my head. I'm not a baby person. I don't have any siblings and haven't spent much time around them. In truth, they make me nervous, like I'm gonna break them or they're gonna explode if I hold them wrong. I'd rather hold a live bomb than a baby, truth be told. At least no one makes you pretend you aren't terrified of a bomb going off. And a bomb doesn't cover you in poop when it explodes.

Sergeant Guinsler hands the snoozing baby back to Lena, who sets him carefully into his carrier again. "We'll be on our way, just as soon as you give this young man some trivia he can use in his report for school."

"Trivia, huh?" She thinks a moment, and then it dawns on her. "Did you know the original plan for this building was as a temporary headquarters for the War Department during World War Two?"

"Kind of a big building to be temporary," I point out.

"They figured after the war, they could use it for file storage. One thing wars generate is a lot of paperwork."

"Six million square feet of paperwork?" I ask.

"Well, I suppose some of it would have remained office space," she says. "None of them saw the digital revolution coming. Your father probably moves more data in a minute than they could've stored here in a year."

"Oh, that's good!" I tell her, jotting it down.

"The battlefield of the future is in cyberspace," she says, and then nods toward all the screens and maps in the Navy Command Center. "Of course, we'll still need our ships at sea."

"Hooyah," says Sergeant Guinsler.

"Oorah," Lena replies. I look between them like they're speaking an alien language.

"Oh, finally something he can't figure out!" Sergeant Guinsler jokes.

For a second I wonder if they've both lost their minds or have a secret code or something, like when my friend Patrick and I invented a language in fourth grade that no one else but us could speak, but also that we kind of just made up as we went along. It sounded like a bunch of grunts.

"'Hooyah' is the traditional battle cry of the Navy," Lena explained. "I'm a Navy veteran myself, so Sergeant Guinsler used it to be a smart aleck."

"Or out of respect." He grins. "And 'oorah' is the Marine Corps battle cry, which Lena has no right to use but does it anyway because she's jealous."

"You wish," she says, laughing at him. "Now get out of here and let me work, you two. It's a big building and I've got meetings all morning."

"People sure have a lot of meetings here," I tell them both, thinking about my dad going to a budget meeting while I'm on this tour.

"You know the most common job in the military, Mikey?" Sergeant Guinsler asks me as we weave our way between the cubicles, heading out toward the hallway.

"What's that?"

"A PowerPoint Ranger," he laughs, though I don't get it. It doesn't sound like a compliment though. Sensing my confusion, he explains, "This is a headquarters, not a field base, so most people working here make PowerPoint presentations, organize budgets, and create plans that other people carry out. We're a nation in peacetime, for the most part, so the closest anyone here will get to death and danger is in traffic on the Beltway during their commute. That's not a bad thing though, right? 'Unhappy is the land in need of heroes.'"

"Whoa," I say, pulling out my pad as we walk down the hall toward a set of stairs up to the second floor. "That's deep. Did you make it up?"

"No, that's Bertolt Brecht, a German playwright." He holds the stairwell door open for me. "Don't tell anyone, but I'm a knuckle-dragging jarhead with a library card. I'm even writing a novel, on the sly."

"You? A writer?"

He leads me up to the second floor and down an endless hallway, walking backward as he talks. "Yep, working on a book about my time in the military. Love, loss, and MREs. I'm telling you because I figured you're a reader yourself. Thought you'd be interested."

"I am," I tell him.

"You have a favorite book?"

"*Hatchet* by Gary Paulsen," I say. "I like how the kid survives against impossible odds."

"That's a great book," he agrees. "Now we're going to see someone I think you'll like. Ann is the Librarian of the Army, and like librarians everywhere, she's the closest we have to a superhero. There's nothing she doesn't know or can't find out. If you've got questions, I bet she can point you toward the answers."

"Cool," I say. "I didn't know the Army had librarians."

"Every branch does," he tells me. "This much information, it has to get preserved and organized, or else it'd be chaos. They say an army marches on its stomach, but a superpower triumphs with its information.

Librarians are the guardians of information. Don't let anyone tell you otherwise."

We walk through another huge area of office cubicles, though this one looks like it's just been renovated. The walls are freshly painted and everything smells new. A sign reads DCSPER, for the Office of the US Army Deputy Chief of Staff for Personnel. They probably need a librarian here just to keep track of all the acronyms.

We weave through the maze of cubicles and Sergeant Guinsler glances across it toward a large conference room door. "Looks like General Maude is in a meeting," he says. "Otherwise I'd introduce you. Not every day you get to meet a lieutenant general. He's a good man to know. And a good man in general, no pun intended. But let's find Ann."

We find her clustered with another group of civilian and military employees around a TV. They're all staring at the screen in stunned silence, and I see the image of the World Trade Center again, one of the towers still smoking and smoldering from the airplane accident. The whole top of the skyscraper is on fire, but something doesn't look right. The top of the other tower is on fire too. Has the fire spread?

Someone answers my question before I can ask it.

"A second plane crashed into the other tower," some-one says.

Sergeant Guinsler frowns and then rests a hand on my shoulder, pulling me back. I can't tear my eyes off the screen though. The black smoke billows out from one tower so thickly I can hardly see the building while smoke and red-hot flames erupt from the second tower too. I think I see people falling from the windows.

Someone near me gasps, and I look away, shutting my eyes. It's one thing to read about tragedy, but another to see it right there, live, on a screen. Some things you can't ever unsee.

"We've got to get you back to your dad," the sergeant tells me. "These are no accidents. This is an attack."

SAGE

I smell worry.

I smell fear.

I smell hickory-smoked bacon, egg, and cheese.

My human isn't here, though her smells linger in the air. There are other humans gathered around the television and I can see from my kennel that they're watching something. My human got hurt the other day, and I haven't been able to play with her. Someone else has been playing with me and training with me here at Virginia Task Force 1, Urban Search and Rescue. I like her, though she doesn't have the same easy way with me as my own handler. I see her now with the members of the task force, all of them in their uniforms, and all of them sweating.

I hear the term "called up" a few times and "activated." That means they think they're about to go to work. That means there's been a disaster. That's what they do here, after all. They help when there's been a disaster.

See? Dogs know more than they think we do. At least, I do. They call me Sage, which is a fine name and a delicious smell.

Humans love to talk about how smart their Search & Rescue K9s are, but they think we only know what we're trained to know. We're dogs and we've been training alongside humans for as long as humans have been walking upright. I'm a border collie. My ancestors were bred to herd sheep and assist humans in every aspect of tending their flocks. It's not an exaggeration to say that humans would never have mastered livestock if it weren't for dogs like me. And thanks to that lineage, I'm one of the great working-dog breeds in the world. If a person needs something amazing—almost impossible—done by a dog, chances are they'll look to a dog like me.

But even the lowliest among us can see and hear and think and smell more than humans realize. Every one of us knows more about people than people can possibly imagine.

For example, I know when my usual handler has been riding her horse, just by the smell of it, and I know how long it's been since she's come to the kennel by the way her smell lingers in the air. Every day she isn't here, her smell fades just a bit. We dogs can tell the passage of time with our noses.

I also know that these humans are on edge. We work for the Federal Emergency Management Agency, stationed in Fairfax, Virginia. When something bad happens and people need help, they turn to us, our teams of humans and dogs, to find people in need of rescuing.

It's a super-important job, and the other dogs who've deployed on rescue missions always come back smelling of smoke and sweat and treats and triumph. They're always a little puffed with pride afterward, like their tails have been dipped in peanut butter.

I haven't had a chance to do anything like that yet. I've been training for it my whole life, or at least since I was a puppy. I'm two years old now though, not a puppy anymore. I'm ready for a real mission. I've learned how to search an area, following the cone of a scent to its source even when there are distractions and rubble and ruins in the way. I've learned how to separate thousands of human smells from each other, so that I can find a specific person even when there are dozens around me. I can find a person who isn't even breathing anymore, and who needs help fast.

I can find a person who is past helping, who hasn't breathed for a long time, by the smell of the decay and the bacteria.

Yeah, dogs know about bacteria. Humans don't think we do, but we can smell those invisible bits of life. We have to. That's how we know when something's food or not, alive or not, friend or foe or frightening. I mean, a person can carry around two pounds of bacteria in their body at any time. Some kind of sniffer I'd be if I couldn't smell it, right? Leave two pounds of steak out and try to keep a dog from smelling it!

Anyway, I know that I finished something important the last time my handler was here, because I did a training in front of a lot of other people, and they all cheered when I finished with my last alert. I found the sock they'd buried in a box, telling them exactly where to find it by sitting and barking. That means I'm ready to deploy just like the other dogs when there's a mission that needs me.

I can tell by the smells of sweat and adrenaline wafting in the air that the day might be today. I can't see much, but from the humans around the television set I hear the words "fire" and "skyscraper" and "rescue operation." And even more ominously, "cadaver," which is a word humans use to describe a dead body when they're trying not to get too upset about it.

The thing is, they're always upset about that word. I can smell their upset-ness. It smells like salt and moldy onions and metal. It has a tang and it makes me want to sit down next to them and rest my head on their lap and let them scratch behind my ears. Humans love scratching behind a dog's ears when they're sad. It's how we've trained them to manage their feelings. Dogs are good at managing humans' feelings for them. Dogs are good at just about everything, in my opinion. I lack thumbs, but I don't lack confidence.

Suddenly, the worry smell intensifies across the room, like someone just tore open a bag full of raw fear and sadness and excitement, and I know something big is happening. Really big.

"Oh my God," says one of the humans at the TV.

"A second plane?" gasps another.

"This isn't an accident," says my substitute handler. "Those planes were crashed on purpose."

I can smell sleep on her too. She was woken up suddenly to come in to work today. It's early in the morning; there's a morning crispness in the air and I've only just been fed. The humans are looking at their clocks and figuring out how long it will take to get to whatever place this airplane accident or attack or whatever they're calling it happened.

"People would've been at work already," someone says.

"Those poor people could be trapped," says someone else.

"I think we better get ready," says a third person, who always smells a little like cinnamon, which is not my favorite smell. It's really strong and it makes me sneeze.

"To New York?" my temporary handler asks.

I don't know where New York is, and a whine escapes me. I can't help it. I blame the cinnamon. My eyes dart around the kennel and my nose works the air. My usual handler isn't here and the thought of going on my first mission to some unfamiliar place without her makes me nervous. I can tell the other K9s in their crates are sniffing in my direction, smelling *my* fear. I pant, which calms me down a bit, and wait. There's nothing to do but wait, really. I'm a well-trained, newly certified, two-year-old search and rescue professional. Even if I'm afraid, I will not let my fear stop me from doing my job, wherever it takes me and whatever we find.

"If this is an attack," says the man who all the other humans usually take instructions from—I guess he's *their* handler—"then we don't know where we'll be needed. There could be other targets. This could be nationwide."

"Turning airplanes into bombs . . ." my handler sighs. "Dreadful."

I know what a bomb is, because I've been trained to know what some of them smell like, but I've never been sure what they're for. They seem to cause only death and destruction. Dogs like me are only called in *after* a bomb goes off. There are other dogs trained to find bombs before they go off. Still, I don't think airplanes are supposed to be bombs.

A smell tangy as steel and sharp as lemons fills my nose. It's the smell of resolve. The humans are preparing themselves mentally and physically for whatever is about to happen. Some of them leave the television and begin to pack equipment into bags, preparing for a deployment. I see breathing masks and special suits going into duffel bags, all kinds of detectors and baggies and even the dreaded heavy bags they use for cadavers.

I also see leashes and leads, and goggles and booties

designed just for us dogs. None of us like that stuff very much, but the humans always try to put it on, telling us it's for our safety. I wish they trusted us to decide what was safe for ourselves. We're professionals too, after all.

Still, it's nice they try to protect our paws. They mean well, these humans. Most humans I've met, in fact, mean well.

It's a shame they can be so cruel to each other sometimes.

That's one thing we dogs can never understand.

MIKEY: 9:30 A.M.

We scurry through the maze of second-floor hallways from E-Ring to D-Ring, and I can't help looking around at the worried faces in their cubicles. People are placing urgent phone calls and I catch snippets of them as I walk by.

"Was she at work today?"

"I know, but sometimes you're downtown?"

"He's a firefighter in Staten Island, I'm not sure if he'll be called in."

And those were just the personal calls I heard. There were people making all sorts of work calls too, calls about "force readiness" and "asset deployment" and "defensive postures." People awaiting orders or giving them, hoping for orders, and desperate for information. I remember what Sergeant Guinsler told me about today being an "auspicious" day to be at the Pentagon. Suddenly, it didn't feel so auspicious.

"We'll have to go the long way around the Navy

Command Center," Sergeant Guinsler tells me. "They're going to be busy right now getting reports from all over the world."

We take a stairwell down toward what they called A-E Drive, the road that runs around the middle of all the Pentagon's rings so that cars and trucks and motorized carts can zip more quickly between areas. Some walkways crisscross above us, but the road is pretty quiet right now. Everyone who knows what's happening just got very busy, and anyone who doesn't yet know is already busy doing something else. This is the military's workplace, after all, and in the event of an attack, it makes sense the military gets busy.

Outside, as we make our way toward the door closest to my dad's office, I glance at the sky again and think about all the airplanes flying over the United States. There have to be hundreds, maybe thousands in the air at any time. They're filled with innocent people moving around the country on vacations and business trips and visits to family—and all the other reasons people fly. Do they know what's happening right now?

I've only been on a plane once, two falls ago. I was with my mom in Utah, where she was working as a chef in a restaurant at one of the resorts. It was pretty cool because I got to live on the property and use the pool and stuff whenever I wanted. It was the off-season and there weren't a lot of people around, because it was mainly a place where people went to ski and the weather hadn't turned yet. I was pretty happy, because there were a few other kids there, and everyone was so nice and also, mostly, because my mom actually had a job. She struggled a lot with work because she had addictions, but she'd been clean and sober for a while, and things seemed good.

I didn't know that things weren't actually good at all. This is where Sergeant Guinsler is wrong. I get how the world works, how sometimes there is no logic to what happens. You can be living your life perfectly normally, expecting today to be just like yesterday, having a nice time at the state fair when BAM! Out of nowhere your whole life gets flipped around.

When my mom got arrested again, the judge didn't take it easy on her on account of her being a mother. In fact, he probably was harder on her. She'd been separated from my dad for a while, and he had a good job on the other side of the country, and the school year had only just started, so I wouldn't miss much. It was decided by the court, the social workers, and my dad that he'd be given sole custody of me. From then on, I'd live with him in Virginia.

I got flown across the country to him, and that was my only time on an airplane. I was too sad the whole flight to appreciate how beautiful the clouds looked from above, how the sky was so wide and open. I muttered a polite thanks when the pilot let me in to see the cockpit and gave me a little pin with wings on it. The whole flight crew was super nice, and it wasn't their fault I was such a downer. I hardly paid attention to anyone else in the air with me that day. And in spite of a few sideways looks at my big badge that said I was an "unaccompanied minor" on the flight, no one paid me much attention either. We were all caught up in our own dramas. I don't think it would've occurred to any of us that the machine flying us around could be turned into a weapon. And who could do such a thing? Who would? And how?

The questions rustled around with my memories as I scanned the bright blue sliver of sky above the imposing walls of the Pentagon.

"Um, Sergeant Guinsler?" I ask, hustling along behind the fleet-footed Marine before we get to the door going back inside. "I have a question?"

"Fire away," he tells me, and a flicker of doubt across his face makes me think he regrets the word "fire" after what we'd just seen on TV, the skyscrapers burning in New York City.

"If the US is under attack," I ask, "then aren't we a target here?"

That stops Sergeant Guinsler where he's standing, halfway through the door. He looks back at me, then kneels down so we're at the same level. I'm not, like, small for my age, but he's huge, so he kind of looms in front of me, filling my vision.

"This building is full of people who are working day and night to protect everyone in this country," he tells me. "And that includes protecting the people in this building. I promise you, no one is going to let you get hurt."

"But it might not be up to them, right?" I say. "I mean, like, the crew on those airlines wanted to protect everyone on board, but they crashed anyway."

"We don't know what happened yet."

"But—"

He holds up a hand to stop me. "One of the first rules you learn in a crisis is not to let your imagination run away with you. I need you to follow that rule now, okay? You're a smart guy, and that can be a double-edged sword. Focus on what you know and what you can do, not on the tales that impressive brain of yours can spin out, okay?"

I meet his eyes, my so-called impressive brain spinning out a million terrible tales. But I take a breath and stop myself. I nod.

"Oorah," I tell him, which earns a smile. He stands again, leading me inside to find my dad.

"Eden, you seen Dave?" he asks a woman in the next cubicle over when we don't find him at his desk.

"He's still in the budget meeting," Eden says. "This his son?"

"Mikey," I introduce myself.

"Eden," she says, smiling. "Like the garden." Then she cocks her head at Sergeant Guinsler. "Did you see—?"

"Yeah," he cuts her off. "We saw."

She shakes her head. "Maintenance called up; they want to get into the SCIF to make sure the backup servers are getting the right power distribution."

"Now? During this?" Sergeant Guinsler asks.

"I don't make the maintenance schedule," she says. "They can't go in unescorted."

"Affirmative." Sergeant Guinsler sighs and looks back at me. "Looks like duty calls. You gonna be okay waiting at your dad's desk?"

"Sure," I say, a little anxious to be left alone right now, and feeling kinda silly. Everyone here has something important to do, and I'm just standing around.

I'm used to getting shuffled around and handed off among concerned adults, but that doesn't mean it feels good. I know my dad's just in a meeting down the hall, but I still can't shake the feeling that it's a crisis. In times of crisis, I get passed around like an afterthought. I'm a low priority in these moments, always left waiting for the grown-ups to sort out their messes.

Sergeant Guinsler leaves me at my dad's cubicle and I'm alone *again*. I pull out my notebook to jot down thoughts about what this is like, the crackle in the air, the weirdly bland-looking offices where military personnel and civilians are mounting a response to an attack by unknown enemies. A historic day in a historic building, and how I'm on the sidelines of it. Watching it unfold on a dozen little screens scattered among the desks and in the break rooms. I listen to more phone calls.

"I need sitrep on the data centers in WTC," someone says.

"Bank of America's in there too," someone tells them, and the first speaker adds into the receiver, "and financial data. Is someone considering the banks as the target?"

"The Port Authority of New York and New Jersey offices!" the second person hollers.

"Can you please not yell a list of tenants in my ear?" the first person says, in a scolding voice that all middle schoolers know. They both lower their voices so I don't hear any more of their conversation.

Tempers are flaring and no one actually knows anything about what's happening in New York. The tension in my dad's office is so thick I can almost taste it. I see men and women in uniform hustle through the hallways from one meeting room to another. Secretaries at the copy machines watch them pass, just as anxious and hungry for information as I am.

This reminds me of waiting outside the courtroom at my mom's sentencing, before I got flown across the country to my dad. At least then, the social worker sat with me while we waited for my fate to be decided. Here, I'm alone, and it feels like the fate of thousands of people, maybe millions, hangs on what is happening behind closed doors in these meeting rooms and the hundreds of other meeting rooms around the building.

I wonder what all the generals upstairs are doing right now.

I wonder what the firefighters I saw outside the building near the helicopter pad are doing right now.

I wonder what the people trying to get out of the burning World Trade Center towers are doing right now.

I can feel my imagination starting to run away from me. This is what it must've been like during the Cold War, when everyone thought the Soviets had nuclear weapons aimed at this building. People going about their business, doing their jobs, always with the sense that death could fall from the sky at any moment.

The feeling isn't doing my bladder any favors.

I pop up and make my way out to the hall between C and D Rings to find the men's room. I catch a glimpse of a clock as I go past: 9:34 a.m. It's been, like, an hour since that first plane flew into the first skyscraper in New York. I hope all the people have made it out by now.

I have the bathroom to myself, which is nice, because it gives me a chance to splash water on my face when I'm done, to try to calm my nerves.

I take a deep breath, make a brave face in the

mirror, and step back out into the hall to go back to my dad's office. When he comes out of his meeting, I think I'm going to ask if we can go home. I have enough info to finish my report, and today doesn't seem like a good day to be at the Pentagon anymore. Everyone is busy and I'll just be in the way. I don't want to be a kid who gets in anyone's way, who messes things up. I've been that kid before, the day my mom got arrested and—I stop myself. I really don't want to think about that day right now.

Instead, I rehearse a little speech about the reasons to tell Dad he should let me go home on the Metro all by myself. I'm idly playing with my visitor's badge, which I realize says that I need an escort with me at all times, but in the chaos of the morning, I seem to have been let loose without one. If someone catches me, will they think I'm a spy? Will I be arrested like the badge says?

I look around anxiously. Sergeant Guinsler had said something about the badges being alarmed. I worry if I take one wrong step, sirens will blare and guns will be drawn on me.

I see a uniformed soldier walking in my direction from the doorway to the Navy Command Center, and

I'm afraid I'm about to get in trouble. No alarms are sounding, but he looks agitated.

I figure I can avoid the trouble if I ask him for directions first, even though I totally know where I'm going. You can really take the anger out of a grown-up by asking them for help before they can ask you what on earth you think you're doing.

"Excuse me, sir!" I call, hoping I didn't just offend another enlisted man by calling him sir like he's an officer. He stops and looks at me, frowning. "I was wondering if you could—"

I don't get my question out, because before I can finish, the world explodes around us.

MIKEY: 9:37 A.M.

When I was eight, I flipped over the handlebars of my bike going way too fast over a pothole that was way deeper than I thought. I remember how I saw the hole coming and time slowed. I felt the impact, felt myself leave the bike seat. I rolled forward, headfirst, doing a full flip before I crashed into the pavement and slid, my bike landing on top of me. The crash probably took two seconds, but it moved in slow motion. It felt like hours until the pain snapped me back to the present and the taste of my own blood made me cry out for help.

This is a lot like that. Time slows so that I can see everything happening, but it also turns to jelly, too thick to move through. I can't do anything about it.

There's a huge boom, louder than any sound I've ever heard in my life. I feel the building shudder. The floor ripples, and my first thought is *earthquake*, but there are no earthquakes in Northern Virginia.

At the same time I have that thought, I try to hold

myself up while the floor moves away from my feet. The air behind the uniformed soldier at the end of the hall shimmers. There's a heat wave behind him, rippling like a mirage in the desert. It fills the huge hallway from floor to ceiling and my brain can't make sense of it. Did we get hit by a tidal wave?

The soldier has this surprised expression on his face, and then the shimmering air around him bursts into flame, a sheet of fire that covers him completely. The flash of light nearly blinds me and the sudden heat scalds my face.

Where the soldier had been standing in the door to the Navy Command Center, a blast of fire and wind punches out, knocking the breath from my lungs and throwing me off my feet.

I want to shout, but I've got no air to shout with. I feel like I'm drowning in the hallway, tumbling ahead of a roaring inferno. I don't even know where my limbs are going, whether the floor is up or down. Everything's a jumble, like reality has become unstitched, and suddenly the lights go out. It's pitch black. I feel myself hit something hard, smacking me forward again. My own lights go out then.

When I come to, my ears are ringing, my eyes sting,

and my throat feels like I've just swallowed a can full of rusty nails. I gasp for air and barely get any. What I do breathe in tastes like ash and sulfur and gas. My eyes struggle to focus on the dim light of the hall. The light is coming, I suddenly realize, from the fire licking the ceiling above me. It's like the surface of a red-hot ocean, undulating, almost alive. Ceiling tiles drip, melting like ice cream. For a moment my confused brain wonders why my body feels cool while my face feels so hot. Am I lying in a pool of ice cream?

I look down the length of my body, terrified I'll find some mangled mess of charred flesh and blood-soaked khaki pants. I even fear the shame that I might've peed myself, but what I see instead is that I'm soaked from the chest down by a fire sprinkler dousing me with lifesaving water.

I push myself farther into its spray, so my face and hair are wet and cool too, cleaning out the dust and debris from my eyes. The air around the water steams, especially up by the pipe on the ceiling, which is now surrounded by fire. I watch as the metal of the pipe starts to melt and bend, like in *Terminator 2* when the robot made of liquid metal changes form.

The sprinkler drips molten metal that sizzles as it

hits the floor, and soon the water stops flowing.

I can't make any sense of what I'm seeing. It's a nightmare. Where walls once were, there is now only rubble. Where the ceiling had been is flame and black smoke. I look in what I think is the direction I'd been facing, toward the Navy Command Center. I see a mountain of debris, chairs and desks and pieces of steel and concrete, like they've all been thrown around by a giant toddler having a tantrum.

There are wires dangling, hissing, shooting sparks, and I'm suddenly very aware that I'm in a puddle of water. If one of those hits the water all over the floor, that'll be it for me. My body moves before my brain even tells it to.

I'm up off the ground, running in the other direction, away from the wall of fire and the wires and the melting sprinkler system, but I can't stand all the way up. The smoke is too thick at the height of my head, the heat too intense. I have to duck down. I'm on all fours, scrambling over sharp edges, broken plastic, and glass. It's dark again, and the rubble shakes underneath me. I know I'm climbing up a pile of something, because I can feel my feet slipping down as I go.

It's another mountain of sharp debris, and I'm

pretty sure I cut my knee on it. It's hotter near the top. The air is impossible to breathe. I pull my wet shirt up over my mouth and nose to gasp through the fabric. It helps. In front of me, I feel something like the broken wall of a cubicle lying on its side. Weirdly, it still has thumbtacks in it, and in the dim light I can make out photographs pinned to it, though they're charred.

The heat at the top of this rubble pile scorches my back. I feel like it might be burning me alive. I can't stay this close to the ceiling much longer. I have to get down, get low, and find a way out.

I slide myself onto the top of the broken cubicle wall and shove it, using it like a sled to slide down the other side of the mountain of rubble. I slam to a stop against a heap of office furniture that's completely twisted and broken—and on fire. I gasp, rolling off my improvised sled and crashing to the floor below. There, I see a burning upside-down conference table.

Beyond it, I can just make out the cavernous office space I'd rolled into.

I don't know where I am. The building I'd been writing a report on, the building whose maps I'd studied and whose hallways I'd explored, was now unrecognizable. I'm not sure I even know where the exit doors are anymore, but I think I'm pointing in the direction of C-Ring, which opens onto A-E Drive, where there will be fresh air to breathe and, hopefully, people to help me. The more I come back to my senses, the more my whole body hurts. I'm in some trouble here.

It feels like a year has passed since I called out to that soldier in the hallway, but it's probably been less than three minutes.

I hear an explosion in the far distance, and at least I know the ringing in my ears didn't take my hearing away. I can see. I can hear. I can feel. I'm alive. I have no idea what's happening, but I am alive. My heart pounds in my chest. I stop to listen, to breathe. I think about the boy in *Hatchet*, how he wants to panic, but he has to stay calm and think in order to survive.

If I want to survive, I have to think.

Except, in thinking, I'm now too aware of time passing, too aware of every panicked thought in my head. My imagination starts to run away from me. Did a bomb go off? Is the building under attack? Is America being invaded right now? I don't see any other people, so I start to fear I'm the only survivor. I imagine zombie movies, end of the world movies, movies where I have to fight an invading army by myself, hand to hand in the flame and fire, just to stay alive.

That's when I remember what Sergeant Guinsler told me, the first rule you learn in a crisis. Don't let your imagination run away with you. Focus on what you know and what you can do, not what scares you, not what you imagine. What is real and what is happening right now.

Right now, the building is on fire.

Right now, it's getting harder and harder to breathe.

Right now, I'm on my belly, looking through the dark toward what used to be the main floor of the Navy Command Center.

I thought I'd been going in the whole other direction. I was so turned around in my panic, I'd actually circled back somehow to what looks like the site of the explosion. Where there had been rows and rows of cubicles and high-tech screens for monitoring ships and aircraft all over the world, there is now just chaos.

Focus on what I know.

People worked here. A lot of them. There's no way I'm the only one left. I have to find them. Maybe they can help me. Maybe I can help them.

I find my voice and call out, "Hello!" It comes out like

a raspy whisper. I try again. "HELLO! ANYONE THERE!"

"Over here!" someone screams. "Help! I'm stuck! I can't find him! I can't—!" The voice cracks, but even through the ringing in my ears, I recognize it. It's Lena, who I met before. I crawl toward the voice, and that's when I see what she's screaming about.

Her baby carrier is blown over on its side beneath the rubble. My stomach lurches into my throat.

There's no baby in it.

"I have to find him!" Lena screams, and I forget all about the pain I'm in, or my hurt knee, or the ringing in my ears. There's a baby missing in this burning rubble, and I have to help find him, before the fire burning the ceiling kills us all.

"Don't worry! I'm coming!" I yell, sounding much more confident than I feel.

SAGE

We're on the road, moving north fast, and there are lights flashing on the roof of the truck. We're in a convoy of four trucks, and there's a loud car with flashing red and blue lights leading us so we don't get stuck in traffic.

Most of the traffic is going the other way, I notice, and I can smell the human fear scents over the road like it's smoke from a fire.

I also smell smoke from a fire.

I know we're going north by the way the air smells, and by the way the trees bend and the sun moves. Dogs have a very good sense of direction. We don't need all those gadgets that humans use to find their way. I guess we come with our own gadgets: our ears that pick up on subtle sounds human ears miss and our noses that can smell ten thousand times better than a human's nose can. The part of our brain that makes sense of smells is forty times greater than the part of a human's brain that does that. When a human smells "something gross," I smell a symphony, scents on top of scents, an entire story in a smell.

That's why I make such a good search and rescue dog. I can pick up the smell of a human from miles away. I can smell a person below rubble and wreckage and dirt and mud. I can even smell the difference between a human who is alive and a human who isn't anymore.

Sometimes, in training, it gets frustrating when I can't find any of the smells I'm supposed to, but I don't get distracted. When some dogs get frustrated, they bark or paw at the ground even though they haven't found what they're looking for, just to try to get a reward. But I never do that. I stay focused, even when I'm super-duper frustrated and can't smell any trace of a person. I know that I can look back at my handler, who will point me in another direction, help me find the cone of smell again, and weave my way down it through the air until I find where it's coming from.

That's how smells work. It's like a funnel. Something lets off its scent into the air, and the smell expands and spreads out, growing fainter the farther it gets from its source. The farther away it is, the wider the area where the tiny scent particles are. So a dog has to pick up the scent and then weave back and forth to see where it's getting stronger, and the cone narrows. Of course, there isn't ever just one smell, so the cones of scent cross each other, intersect, mix and bend and change with the wind. It takes a lot of time and practice to find the right scent cone and stick with it, let it guide you right to the stinky source where it's strongest. When a well-trained dog like me gets there, they bark and paw or sit or lay down—whatever signal they've taught their handler to recognize. Then the humans come and pull out what they've found, whether it's what they call evidence or a cadaver. Or a living, breathing person who needs help and who never would've gotten it without a dog like me.

Except there is no dog just like me, because I'm one of the best there is.

With patience, I know I can *always* find what I'm looking for. In spite of how nervous these humans in all the trucks are, I can't wait to show off my skills on a real search and rescue mission. The other dogs in my kennel are going to roll over with admiration by the time I'm done.

After a while, the traffic along the road thins out, and the only other cars we see are working vehicles with lights flashing and sirens that make me want to bark. (Though I don't, because I know that's rude and confusing to the humans and they've taught me only to bark when I have something to tell them or am just really, *really* happy.) The smells in the air are even stronger now. There are so many sizzling the air that it makes me dizzy. I'm starting to get a sense of the story that's unfolding, just from the smells. It's not a nice story.

There was some sort of crash, because I smell fuel and fire and a few kinds of burning metal. There are plastic smells and rubber smells, and tangy acidic smells I can't quite identify. And then there are the smells of burning paper, wood, fabric, charred stone, and steel. The things humans make smell different when they burn than the things nature makes. That's why rescuing someone in the woods is easier than in a city. I can smell a plane crash among oak and maple and beech trees the way a human can see a flare gun erupting in a clear blue sky. I also know how flare guns smell.

In a city—or what my people at the Federal Emergency Management Agency call an "urban environment"— the smells are more human-made and there are *a lot* of them. It's hard enough to tell them apart when they're not all burning, but just after a fire, it gets a lot

MIKEY: 9:40 A.M.

The smoke above me is thick and black, swirling like a hurricane cloud trapped under a roof. I can't even see the ceiling past it, but the room is so dark, I probably couldn't see the ceiling anyway. It's hard to breathe, even through my wet shirt, and I can feel the air getting hotter and hotter as I crawl forward on my knees and elbows. I sweep rubble out of the way as gently as I can, searching for Lena's baby.

I don't know a lot about babies, but I figure if one got knocked out of a carrier by an explosion, it should be crying. I can hardly think about the reason it's not crying or I might start crying myself.

In fact, I can't think about anything. I just have to keep searching and keep breathing, and those two activities demand all the focus I can muster. The rest of my panicked thoughts will have to wait.

"Zachary!" I hear Lena screaming in the darkness. It

sounds like she's miles away. I guess Zachary is her baby's name.

Her shouting is cut short by a fit of coughing. The air in here is poison.

There are puddles on the floor where I am, water from the broken pipes all around us. "Wet your clothes!" I yell to Lena. "Try to breathe through the wet cloth. It will help!"

"Mikey?" another voice yells in the dark. It's Sergeant Guinsler, though he sounds strange and breathy, like he's cringing and gasping at the same time. "You okay?"

"Yeah!" I yell back, because I don't want to worry him and he sounds not so okay himself. Who could possibly be okay right now?

"You gotta get out of here," he says. "Fire." I know he's talking from somewhere to my left. The heat on that side tells me the fire is probably closer to him than to me, but I also know I'm not going anywhere until Lena and her baby are safe.

I keep moving, trying to make a low circle from where the baby carrier was toward the right. I figure if there was an explosion and fire to the left, the shock wave would've knocked everything rightward, desks and furniture and walls and windows and, yeah, even babies. So I loop around, struggling to breathe through the wet shirt, and keeping my distance from the sizzling wires that dance out of the smoke like snakes in a cursed tomb.

In the distance, I hear a popping sound that I think is gunfire, like we're under attack. I freeze.

"Secondary explosions," Sergeant Guinsler groans in the dark. "Fire spreading."

"I need some help!" a new voice calls out, a man somewhere in front of me. "I'm trapped under a copier!"

I press my forehead to the floor, where it's cooler and the air is a little easier to breathe. I need to think for a second. There are too many people who need help and I'm just one kid crawling on his belly in the dark. I'm not sure what to do and I want to cry. If I could just stay here a second and cry, then maybe someone would come and help *me*. I'm just a kid, right? I shouldn't have to do this. I *can't* do this. I don't even know what I'm supposed to be doing in the first place. I just want my dad.

Dad.

The thought crashes into me like an airplane falling out of the sky.

I need to find my dad's office and make sure he's okay.

I need to tell him that I'm okay.

I can't lie here waiting in the burning dark, or else I'll never get that chance. I have to move, I have to take action, and I have to get out of here, like Sergeant Guinsler said.

I start to crawl in the direction that feels cooler, which I figure is the most likely way out, when something snags me, stops me moving.

It's nothing physical that stops me. I get snagged on that voice in my head, the voice we all have that's quieter sometimes and louder others. But it's always there, the voice telling me the right thing to do.

I think about my mom, how she must've had this voice too, but her addictions were louder than it was. They led her to make mistakes, to run away into drinking and pills when she should've been running toward her responsibilities, toward *me*. She didn't listen to that voice in her head. Maybe she felt like she couldn't or maybe she couldn't even hear it anymore, but the choice she did make hurt her and hurt me too, even though it was probably easier at the time.

I can't make the easier choice, the less scary choice.

I told Lena I'd find her baby and I can't run away from that now, no matter how scared I am. I'm smaller than any of these adults, and I can move through this rubble. I have to at least try.

When I moved into my dad's place, I helped him set up my bedroom. There were all these huge boxes for the dresser and the bed and I wanted to arrange them myself. As I went to grab a really big one, he stopped me and said, "You don't have to lift more than you can carry."

He meant it about more than boxes, but I lifted the big box that day anyway. It hurt, but I moved it into place.

And today, this hurts, but I can carry it. I can do this.

I swallow my fear and my panic and my sadness, and I turn again toward the heat, continuing my circle, searching and sweeping the ground, straining through every smoky breath.

The wreckage is sharp. Small bits of it cut my forearms as I pull myself along. Anywhere my skin touches feels hot, and I can't tell if the smell of burning hair is coming from me or not. I don't want to think about what else I'm smelling. I wish I could just shut my nose off and not smell at all. My nostrils hurt with the chemical stink around me. If a smell could be translated into a sound, this would be like a death metal concert with no earplugs.

I run into what I think is a desk turned on its side, the metal legs all bent and twisted. I turn to push past it, when I see something in the spot where the drawers should be. One of the deep drawers is still in place. It must have been locked when the explosion happened, but there's an open hole where the lower one had been knocked out and there is something soft in that space, sheltered from the heat and wreckage: a blanket.

My heart jumps and I shove myself forward, thrusting my hands into the opening to grab the lumpy blanket. It reeks of gas fumes and I swipe it away, letting it fall onto the floor as I pull the small squirming thing away from it, curling around and bringing my face close so I can feel the breath of the little baby on my cheek.

"I have him!" I shout as loud as my scratchy throat will let me. "I found your baby! Ms. Lena! I found him!"

The silence that follows lasts seven breaths. I count each one of them, ears buzzing, heart thundering, a tiny baby cradled against me. I'm curled over him like a turtle shell, like my fragile flesh and bones could protect this infant if the Pentagon came down around us.

Which it might.

"I'm coming!" Lena finally shouts. "Keep making noise so I can find you!"

"Over here! Right here!" I yell, but it's really hard and I can't catch my breath. I guess the yelling was scary though because that starts the baby crying, and I'm glad for it. Every mother in the world will find her way to the sound of her own baby crying, no matter the dark or the danger. Even my mother.

I picture my mother's face in the dark now, imagine that it's her crawling through the burning rubble to save *me*.

"I'm coming, baby!" Lena calls out to her infant son. I imagine her voice is my mom's voice, calling out to me. It makes me feel brave.

Except my mom's locked up on the other side of the country and I'm far from safe. Does she even know what's happening here? Does she worry about Dad and me? Is the whole country under attack? Will the guards even tell her what's going on?

I want to be there when she gets out. I want to tell her what I did today. I want to survive this.

Just then, something stings me. It feels like a bee, except that makes no sense.

I look up and see the ceiling drip. The fire is turning the ceiling tiles into boiling liquid. I feel it sizzle where it plops on my back, burning right through my shirt. I grit my teeth and try not to let out one of the seven worst curse words I know, because I don't think I should curse in front of a baby. My dad once told me that there's a time and a place for everything, even curse words, and growing up is learning to judge for yourself when that time and place is. *"If you think it might be the wrong time, then you're probably right. Trust your instincts, kiddo. You know more than you think."*

The sizzling pain brings tears to my eyes, but it keeps me from thinking too hard about my mom or dad.

Suddenly, Lena is there, and she's taking her son from my hands. She's crouched with me, rocking him, cooing to calm him, but she sits up higher than me and is quickly doubled over coughing from the smoke. The building rumbles. I hear crashing, breaking glass. Is the Pentagon coming down around us, or just burning up with us in it?

Neither option is good and both are possible.

"We have to stay near the floor," I tell her. "Do you know a way out?"

"I think so," she says, and points in what I think is the direction I came from.

I shake my head. "That way's blocked. I think the explosion started there."

"Head to the interior!" Sergeant Guinsler calls out from the dark. "Remember A-E Drive?" A fit of coughing cuts him off, and for a moment I worry he died, but he starts up again. "I can see light that way, a hole in the building. You can get out. Go now!"

"What about you?" I yell back.

"Mikey, go!" he replies.

"And the guy under the copier?" I yell. "You still there?"

No reply comes. My gut twists. I know what no reply means.

"Mikey, there is no time! Get out of there!" Sergeant Guinsler bellows.

I look at Lena. She's bent down, holding her baby against her, and I can see that she's favoring one leg. Her outfit is scorched and there are burns on one side of her face and shoulder. There's no way she can make it through this wreckage alone to the hole in the wall that Sergeant Guinsler is talking about.

This isn't a choice a kid should have to make, but then again, it's not much of a choice at all.

I have to go with her and the baby. I have to get them to safety.

I have to leave Sergeant Guinsler behind.

MIKEY: 9:45 A.M.

We slither along the floor in the dim light. I hear distant fire alarms and some sort of muffled announcement, but I can't even begin to make out what it's saying. Whatever emergency fire systems the Pentagon has in place aren't working in this part of the building, probably because they're all melted. The sprinklers in this room aren't even on.

Not that it matters, because it's not the fire that's most dangerous for us right now. It's the smoke. It keeps getting thicker and thicker, so black I can see its darkness even in the dark. It's as low as the desks and we have to stay almost lying down just to breathe. Even the clear air by the floor is chunky as chicken soup.

The heat down at the floor makes it feel like I'm standing too close to a bonfire trying to roast a marshmallow, except *I'm* the marshmallow. The flames aren't even all that close to me. It's so hot that I can feel my skin scalding, and steam rises from my soaked clothes.

This room is not going to be survivable much longer. At least the kid in *Hatchet* only had to worry about himself. I'm frightened for Lena and her baby too.

We crawl along the floor and the building rumbles above us. Weirdly, there's a desk right in front of me that hasn't moved at all. It's covered in dust and bits of debris, but it's otherwise untouched while everything around it is in shambles. The computer is still in its spot, plugged in to nothing. The chair is pushed in and there's even a mug filled with pens, totally undisturbed. A light sweater hangs off the back of the chair. I pull it down, giving it to Lena to wrap her child in for extra protection against the smoke and sharp edges all around us. She coughs as she nods to thank me.

We rest for a moment at the desk, where the air is slightly cooler, like it's a bus shelter in a summer storm. I don't know how a blast radius works, or how shrapnel spreads, but somehow this one piece of boring office furniture dodged the utter destruction around it, through a trick of physics or luck or fate.

I'm not sure why, but I feel like this desk means we're headed in the right direction. It's like a sign: If a desk can survive here, maybe we can too.

I'm grasping for meaning where there maybe is

none, but I need something to keep me going. Otherwise I'll start thinking about that man under the copier and his silence, or about Sergeant Guinsler, trapped somewhere in the inferno, and then I won't be able to keep going.

Just because there's fear in my stomach and pain in my body and doubt in my mind doesn't mean I have to listen to any of it. *I* decide what I do, not my fears and not these fires. Nothing will stop me, not even myself. I take the deepest breath I can, which hurts and makes me cough some more, but I get enough air to keep moving. The smoke is so thick even two feet off the ground that I don't think I'd last a minute trying to breathe it. At least against the floor, I can see a little bit to make our way.

Without a word, we crawl on, though both of us could've used more rest. We have no time. Every second that passes the air gets hotter and harder to breathe. My visibility keeps getting worse too and my eyes burn. I have no idea how the rest of the huge building is doing, but if it's anything like the Navy Command Center, the casualties are going to be horrific. I think of the twenty thousand people who work here. How many are dead or dying right now?

I want to throw up, but I'm determined that this woman, this baby, and I will not be among the dead. Not here. Not today.

We press on, gasping through thin cloth, fighting for every breath like we're mountaineers trying to summit Everest. It takes what feels like forever to reach what I think is the inner wall of C-Ring, though there is a literal mountain of rubble in the way and I'm not certain exactly where we are.

The air feels a tiny bit cooler here, and brighter, and when I look toward the top of this rubble heap, I can see light. It's not the terrifying blue-orange glow of fire but a gentle white gleam and a stream of thick black smoke pouring out above it.

"Daylight!" I shout, which sets Lena's baby crying again, which gives me an idea. I shout louder. "If you can hear my voice or the baby crying, head this way! There's daylight! Sergeant Guinsler!"

"I hear you, Mikey," he calls back. "I'll do my best. Now, go!"

I scuttle to the side to help Lena forward ahead of me.

I start to turn. I *can* go back to get Sergeant Guinsler now that I know the way out. It had taken a long time to get here, but I could do it again. My knee hurts and my lungs are burning. My throat's scratchy and my eyes feel like they're filled with sand. Even my sweat hurts where my skin is raw from the heat, but I'm certain I can make it back to where I'd come from, find the sergeant, and escort him out the same way. A Marine never leaves a man behind, and though I'm not yet a man, I'm not going to leave a Marine behind.

Lena starts to crawl up the mountain of broken steel and glass and concrete and plastic with one arm around her baby, which makes for unsure footing. She stumbles on the first steps up, as the rubble shifts. I freeze, watching her struggle, and my heart sinks.

My work is not yet done.

I go to her side, taking her arm to stabilize her, and help her, step-by-step, up the mountain.

By the time we reach the top, we're both gasping and the baby is coughing and wheezing a little. The daylight is so bright it's blinding, but I immediately know I won't make it back down into the room again. The smoke is already belching out thick behind us. Looking back, I can't even see the way we came from. Even just turning to look makes me flinch because the air is so hot on my face. The fire's growing, spreading, and now, from up here, I know why.

Everything smells like jet fuel.

I know the smell. I remember it from the tarmac, waiting to take off on the flight that took me to the East Coast, away from my mother, toward my father. Toward this day. Toward right now.

A plane has crashed into the Pentagon, just like at the World Trade Center, and I'm standing on a pile of rubble in a hole in the wall made by the force of that explosion.

I'm dimly aware of people in uniform rushing to Lena, escorting her down the pile into the open air of the wide A-E drive. Someone gives her oxygen, which she's trying to give to her baby instead, though the mask doesn't fit. A few sailors are yelling, waving to get a medic's attention, and my companions from the rubble are led away without another look back. I'm frozen still, staring at the clear blue sky, grateful it's still there, grateful I'm seeing it again and gulping air from it.

But I don't feel safe.

My watch still works. It's 9:49 in the morning. It's only been about ten minutes since the explosion.

The clear sky over me suddenly feels like a threat.

As someone takes my arm and leads me away from the huge hole in the side of the building, I'm still looking up, wondering how many more planes are up there and if any more are headed this way.

MIKEY: 9:52 A.M.

A-E Drive is chaos. I glance toward the hole I just came through and see a blown-out window on the second floor, just as someone jumps from it into the arms of the huge officer below. I can hear the thump of impact as the man catches the jumper and they both hit the ground, winded but alive.

Or, at least, I think alive.

I can't tell if the person who'd jumped from the window is a man or woman, Black or white, old or young, civilian or military . . . anything. They look like charcoal in human form, blackened and burned all over, and the man on whom they landed is immediately rolling them around, patting the flames out. Before I can see anything else, more people have scooped the burned person up onto a stretcher made out of what used to be a door, and are carrying them away in a hurry.

I get my bearings and see that people are everywhere now.

Lena and I hadn't come through that huge hole in the first-floor wall alone after all. People are still climbing out behind where we were, though I hadn't seen or heard any of them inside. Maybe they couldn't talk or maybe I'd just been so focused on my own situation, I hadn't noticed anyone else's. I've heard that in a crisis it can be dangerous to get what they call "tunnel vision," where you only see a narrow point directly in front of you and can't glimpse the bigger picture. I thought I'd been so clearheaded in there, but now I know I hadn't seen anything clearly. There are so many more people who need help—and also more people helping. A whole line of soldiers, sailors, Marines, and civilians has formed at the top of the rubble heap, and they're pulling people out and passing them down to volunteers on the ground.

I shiver, feeling suddenly cold.

I just climbed that way, I think. *Did I climb over all those people without even seeing them?*

I notice to my left what looks like part of a huge truck tire, which takes me a second to recognize as a piece of landing gear from a jet. I'm still staring at it, puzzling it out, when I notice that someone is talking to me. Someone has *been* talking to me.

"Kid!" she says. "Are you hurt? Are you breathing okay?"

It's a woman with her hair in a tight ponytail. She's in a khaki shirt with ribbons and insignia on it, so I think she's a Navy officer. But I don't really know. She's taller than I am, and she bends down to look me in the eyes. Her eyes are kind but worried.

"Who are you here with? Are you in a school group? Where is your escort?" She taps the plastic badge around my neck. I'd forgotten I was wearing it. When I look down, I'm shocked to see the plastic is bent and melted. Suddenly, I notice the pain in my neck from where the little metal necklace that held it had been digging into me all this time. Maybe even burning me.

"My escort," I say, my thoughts jumbled. I'm supposed to be with my escort. Sergeant Guinsler or my dad. But I'm alone. I'm unauthorized to be alone here, and I worry that she's going to think I'm involved, that I set off the bomb or something.

Except I'm still looking at the huge piece of landing gear and I know it wasn't a bomb that went off. It was a plane crash. A plane crashed into the Pentagon and tore through the three outer rings all the way here, to

A-E Drive, and I'm standing here without my escorts because I left them inside.

"My dad!" I suddenly say. "And Sergeant Guinsler! He's alive. He's right in there!"

I've snapped back to my senses and I start to move toward the rubble pile to get back inside to help them. The officer grabs me, pulls me back.

"You can't go in there," she says. "You need to evacuate to the parking lot. They'll—"

She gets cut off by a shout for help from the rubble pile. A group of men are digging on the heap right where I'd climbed down, and they've uncovered an arm. I gag and cough again, thinking of the horror I'm about to see, but the arm is attached to a body, a man in a suit, who they're digging out of the heap. His head is slumped over and his face is bloody, but he seems to be alive.

My stomach unknots. Warmth floods me. *It's Dad!*

I start toward him, but then he lifts his head. He's not my father, just another guy in a suit. So I stay put as the officer runs over, identifying herself as a medic. She shines a tiny penlight into the man's eyes, working with the rescuers to get him out of the rubble. She's already forgotten me, because I'm not critically injured. I guess in a crisis like this, a kid all alone isn't as much of a priority if he isn't, like, immediately in danger of dying. At least no one thinks I'm part of an attack.

At another hole in the wall near the big one I'd scrambled from, a group of men are going back inside. One or two of them have painter's masks on; others have wrapped wet cloth around their faces. I can tell by the soot on some of their clothes that they've been inside already. They know what they're doing, and most have military haircuts. These are the sort of guys who run into danger to help people. Maybe they can help Sergeant Guinsler. Maybe they can find my dad.

"I know where there's a survivor," I say, running over to them. "At least he was alive a few minutes ago."

A man in an Air Force uniform looks me up and down quickly, and I see his rank is lieutenant general. He's also got a medical symbol on his uniform. A general who's also a doctor. He's just what I need right now.

"Sir," I say, because I know that officers, unlike enlisted Marines, like to be called sir. "There's an

injured Marine I had to leave behind. He was somewhere in the Navy Command Center in all the cubicles.
I think he's hurt. His name is Sergeant Guinsler. If
you're going in, he needs help."

The lieutenant general nods at me and then passes
the info to the guy waiting to go inside. One soldier
comes out, coughing and carrying an injured woman
on his back, passing her down to the next person in
line. The third person moves forward with a flashlight
and his shirt over his nose and mouth. He scurries in,
beneath the thick smoke.

After what feels like forever, but is probably only
about three minutes, he comes out again. His face is
black with grime that's cut by sweat lines, so he
looks like a horror movie zebra-human experiment
gone wrong. He looks at the lieutenant general and
shakes his head. "Can't get any farther in. Can't
even see."

Rescuers are starting to move away from the holes
in the walls. There are no more people crawling
out, and going back in through these holes doesn't
seem like an option. There's rubble everywhere on
A-E Drive, but I know there are doors into Corridor
Four and Corridor Five. Maybe we can get in that

way. My dad's office was right near the Corridor Five exit, so if he got out, he might still be there. And maybe someone can go in to look for Sergeant Guinsler too.

I run in that direction, dodging people on the ground who are trying to catch their breath—people crying, people just staring, people rushing about to help other people. I dodge debris and equipment and I nearly fall flat on my face tripping over a blown-open suitcase with *Toy Story 2* on it and I think, *Why would someone in the Department of Defense have a* Toy Story 2 *suitcase?*

Then I remember the plane. This must have been on the plane that crashed into the building. A *kid's* suitcase.

Right then, I want to throw up. I fall to my knees, which hurts, and my imagination starts to run away from me again. I used to have a Power Rangers suitcase the same size as this one. I took it on the flight to live with my dad. I wonder where the kid on this flight was going?

I'm about to start sobbing, but the sight of firefighters coming down A-E Drive brings my focus back to the present. I take as deep a breath as I can, though the air smells foul. I can't focus on the tragedy that's happened; I have to focus on the work ahead and on all the people trying to help. I have a choice to make, to be a victim or a helper right now, and I know what I want to be.

I make my way toward the firefighters, but just then I see someone familiar. It's the skinny guy from my dad's office. He's standing right in front of me, but it's not clear if he even sees me. He's got a faraway look in his eyes, and he's pretty banged up. Torn clothes, a cut on his arm, and he's not putting any weight on one of his legs. Half his face is covered in soot and he's not wearing his glasses anymore.

"Um, sir? Mister . . . um . . . guy?" I call to him. I don't know his name and I can't read his uniform. He stares at me like he's not sure I'm really there.

"We met before. I'm Dave Cutler's son, Mike? Mikey?"

"Mikey . . ." he says absently, like he's not quite sure. He probably can't see me well without his glasses. His eyes aren't really focused and I see that his pupils are huge.

"Have you seen my dad?" I ask.

"He was there . . . He was in the meeting. I was

outside the room. I was just typing. The building shook and then . . ." He shakes his head, looks toward the holes in the side of the wall.

"Did he get out?" I plead. "Is he alive?"

The guy nods. "Alive, yeah. I lost him though. I think he's . . . He's not out . . . I don't think . . . I don't know if . . ."

His voice fades. He looks pale, like a super-unhealthy pale, and I think about the first aid course I took back in Utah. My mom had insisted I learn CPR. I thought she was just being responsible, but I came to learn she wanted me to know what to do if she overdosed, or had an accident or a heart attack while she was on drugs. I was the only person in her life she could count on, so she wanted me to know what to do if her life was in danger.

The thing is, her life *was* in danger. Every time she used, her life was a little more in danger, and so was mine. And no first aid course I took could help her. They didn't teach how to save your mom from herself at the YMCA.

I think back to the CPR class.

The first thing they teach are the ABC's. You check Airway, Breathing, then Circulation (like if someone's bleeding). If that's all okay, then you can start to assess the other problems.

Are there burns that need treatment? Probably, but I can't do anything about that.

Broken bones that need setting? (Also probably, but I'm no help there either.)

Maybe a concussion, maybe muscle or spine injuries, but I can't tell.

What I do recognize now though are the symptoms of shock.

This young soldier from my dad's office is going into shock. His injuries must be worse than they look. His breathing accelerates and I worry he's hyperventilating, like he's gonna pass out.

I move forward and take his hand, and I guide him down first to my level and then until he's lying down on the ground. There's some rubble right near us and I turn him a little—he doesn't weigh much and he doesn't resist at all—so that his feet are elevated. That's one of the first things you should do for someone in shock. If you can safely move them, get their feet up. That helps the blood flow to their important organs so they don't start shutting down. You don't have to be a military medic to know that someone's organs shutting down is not a good thing.

"Help!" I call out. "He's going into shock!"

The lieutenant general is there in a flash. I get the sense he'd been keeping an eye on me, even as he was working to save other people. It's nice to know someone here cares if I'm okay, except now his attention is on the young soldier on the ground. He starts tending to the guy and another soldier comes over to help. They're totally occupied and this guy is getting real, professional, adult help, so I step away.

I find the firefighters again, just down the way, near the door to Corridor Five. They're trying to wrangle a hose from one of the hookups on the drive to spray a fire on the second floor, but it's burning so hot the water just turns to steam on contact.

I jog up to the first firefighter I can find who isn't engaged with the hose work. He's got a mask and breathing tank on, and an axe in his hand, but he's not moving into the building yet. He's looking around, wide-eyed, focused, and assessing the situation but also kind of shocked by what he's seeing.

"I'm okay," I tell him as his eyes land on me. He flinches. I must look kind of frightful myself. I don't want him immediately assessing me for injuries or shock or anything. I don't have time for that. I'm trying to help people—to help my dad and Sergeant Guinsler. If the fire's really as hot as it looks, then we don't have much time.

"There are survivors still inside!" I tell him, shouting in case he can't hear well through his mask. "There's a Marine sergeant stuck in the Navy Command Center. Also, I'm looking for my dad, Dave Cutler. He's a civilian in the . . ." I hesitate. Am I allowed to say he works for the Defense Intelligence Agency? Should I be revealing top-secret info to a firefighter?

Crisis rules, I tell myself. *The old rules don't apply anymore. Maybe they'll never apply again.*

"He's in the DIA offices near Corridor Five right up that way. We have to find him. He's the only person I have left in the world and I—"

"Whoa, kid, you gotta slow down," the firefighter says. He grabs my shoulders, looks me up and down, checking me for injuries like I thought he would. He points away from the burning holes. "I need you to follow the road that way and get out to the parking lot."

His radio buzzes with noise as every firefighter and rescuer with a radio tries to talk at the same time.

He's ignoring it, but both of us hear the next words, a voice cutting through the clutter, yelling in a very un-firefighter-y way.

"We've got another plane incoming!" the voice barks. "All units evacuate! Twenty minutes out!"

The chorus of static starts up again, but we've heard enough.

"You gotta go now!" yells the firefighter, and then he and his crew spread the word and hustle away the guys at the edge of the rubble pile who are still looking for ways into the building.

I look up at the sky, my stomach in my throat. I brace myself. *Another plane incoming?*

If we're still under attack, it's not like I can run anywhere fast enough. If there's another plane incoming, no one is safe—not here on A-E Drive, not in the undamaged parts of the building, and not in the parking lot. When the sky is falling, it's not like you can cover your head and hide under a desk. When the sky is falling, the best thing you can do is be with the people you care about.

Now that no one's watching me again, I move toward the Corridor Five door. I snag a flashlight one of the rescuers left nearby as he went to help someone else.

I glance around the drive and back up at the blue sky, now hazy with smoke. They said twenty minutes. Maybe that's enough time for all of us.

I hope this isn't the last time I see this sky, but if I'm gonna die today, I'm gonna die trying to save my dad.

SAGE

I know we are at the command post, because there is a man in a uniform standing in front of a whiteboard, where another man is making lists with a stinky, squeaky marker the way humans do. Humans love writing things, especially with squeaky markers. It's not a skill us dogs have ever needed, because we remember what's important and can smell whatever we need to know. Humans would probably write down a description of a smell instead of just, you know, *smelling* it.

I know we're in the parking lot, because there are cars and trucks and car-and-truck smells everywhere. People are moving all around, some away from the billowing smoke of the giant building and some toward it. Everyone moving toward it is in a uniform, so I figure these are my colleagues today. It's nice to see their bravery in the face of danger. I've learned that I only need to get nervous when the people around me are nervous, and if they're calm and focused, then I can be too. We take our cues from each other. Sometimes, if I sense they're nervous, I can even calm them with a lick or a nuzzle. I'm good at calming people, and they're good at calming me too. We're a team. We've practiced looking out for each other since ancient times.

Right now, it's the commander of the post who's making me feel calm. He's speaking firmly but quickly to the firefighters around him. Then he finally talks to our team leader, pointing and explaining things. I don't understand everything he's saying and I find it hard to hear through the windows of the truck and the sounds of sirens that are everywhere. There are so many smells and sights, I almost want to curl up in a ball and hide.

But I don't.

I know I can do better than hide.

I stay ready.

Radios chirp and squawk like birds, but none of the people are paying any attention to the noise. Everyone has a job to do and everyone is doing their best at it. I feel a little silly sitting in the back of this truck, panting while I wait for the chance to do what I'm trained for.

Already, I'm trying to sort the smells that are drifting my way. This is something that most humans don't know about dogs: We make plans. We think about the future. I know that if I do certain things, I'll get certain results, and because I know that, I can try to plan for the results I want. I place toys where I can find them again; I sit by doors so I can greet my handler when she comes in; I sniff the air everywhere I go, so I know what to expect. Dogs are hunters and pack animals, and you can't hunt with a pack without making predictions and plans.

So now I am thinking about what happens next.

The humans are setting up areas to treat injured people and to get seriously hurt people into ambulances that zoom away. Firefighters are putting on heavy equipment and moving toward the giant burning building. Men and women with blue sirens on their cars and trucks are trying to organize everyone who isn't a firefighter, to keep them out of the way. It looks like chaos to me, but I know enough about humans who spend all their time trying to rescue people that there is order to the chaos. These humans make plans and predictions too, and they're doing their best right now.

Something changes suddenly though. The commander barks orders and now people are moving away from the huge building faster, even the firefighters. They look up at the bright blue sky, pointing and chattering, and their fear is obvious. The command post is suddenly on the move.

I don't know what they're afraid of, but from the smell of jet fuel in the huge fire, I think it has to do with airplanes.

Just then my temporary handler approaches the truck, along with another member of the FEMA team. They immediately hop in and start to back the truck up.

"You really think there's another plane coming?" the driver asks.

"Who knows?" my handler says. She smells like sandalwood and cut grass and an antiperspirant chemical in her deodorant, and also like coffee and laundry detergent, and the peanuts and chocolate from a granola bar she ate. She always eats those bars; they're one of the main ways I recognize her.

Under it all is still that onion scent of fear.

"It doesn't change our job," she tells the driver as he pulls us up to a place farther from the burning building. The air is a little clearer here, which I appreciate, though it means I have less access to all the smells coming from the disaster, smells I'll need to sort through when I'm inside. "When we get the all clear, we move in to search."

"He ready?" the driver nods toward the back seat—toward me. I perk up and stop panting.

The handler smiles. "Sure he is," she says. "He passed all the certifications and is a top-rated live-find and cadaver dog. If there's anyone to rescue, he'll find them." She lowers her voice into that cooing tone people sometimes use with dogs. "Won't you, good boy? Won't you, Sage? *Yes!*"

I salivate at her "yes" because it's one of my cue words. In training, every time I get a "yes" I get a treat or a game of tug. I can't help but shift on my paws now, expecting one or the other of my favorite things. I even bark to show her I understand the "yes" cue, because people like to know when I understand them. She tosses me a treat, which I catch midair.

Yeah, I'm good like that.

Then she turns around and they sit in silence, watching the sky.

I stare out the window, watching the people, who

are watching the building burn, and waiting for my turn to help. Through the noise, I hear a rumbling and the smell changes a little. I don't know what it means, but I'm sensitive to all sorts of changes, even from this far away. I feel something shift. The fur on my back stands up; my tail tightens and tucks.

This is dog fear, instinctual. I don't always know what causes it, but I know to trust it when I feel it. The sound and the change in smell—the strange shift of atmosphere—is not coming from the sky. I don't hear a plane, though there are firefighters on megaphones announcing that one is inbound, twenty minutes out, and telling people to get away from the building.

But the change is coming from the building itself. The smoke rising from the huge hole gets blacker, thicker. It's not another plane. Something else is wrong.

I let out a whine and my handler looks back at me. I lay down in the back, put my head on my paws, and stare at her, signaling. But she doesn't know what I mean by it and turns back to look at the sky.

"It's okay, Sage," she tries to reassure me. I whine again, because I don't have any other way of telling her, *No, no it's not okay. Something terrible is about to happen. I don't know what it is, but it is not okay at all.*

MIKEY: 10:00 A.M.

I can't go in through the wall.

For one, there are too many people and they'd see me trying. Two, the smoke and the heat are so intense, I'd never make it. I have to go farther in from the worst of the fire and see if I can find my dad's office from the side. The building is still being evacuated, because of the fire and the threat of another airplane crashing into it. I figure people are either going to the huge central courtyard or out to the parking lots from whatever exits aren't blocked by flame and smoke.

Since my dad's office is right near the site of the crash, there's no way he could've gone out through the whole building to the parking lot. And the only way he'd get to the central courtyard from there is by passing through A-E Drive. I'd have seen him; he'd have been near the young soldier, the one in shock, whose desk was near his.

He wasn't there, so that means he's still inside—at

least I think so. And if he's still inside, the best chance I have of finding him is through Corridor Five. I'm heading there now.

No one is coming out, and the one big group of fire-fighters in A-E Drive is focused on getting everyone clear of the building. I seize the opportunity and slip right inside the wide hall.

It's hot and smoky, but not nearly as bad as it was in the command center I'd escaped. It's only been, like, twenty minutes since the explosion, but the world has turned upside down in those twenty minutes. So has the building itself.

I don't quite know what I'm looking at as I creep in below the smoke line. The walls—where there are still walls, anyway—are warped and bowed, almost like waves. Pieces of ceiling are collapsed and parts of the floor are sticking up. Columns and beams lie side-ways or shattered in pieces and there are wires and pipes where there shouldn't be. It doesn't look like a hallway of offices anymore, but like something out of a sci-fi movie.

The smoke is thick on the top half of the hall. As I make my way forward, staying low to avoid the heat, my path is blocked by a solid wall of wreckage that I can't get around. I could try to climb over it, except I can't see the top through the smoke. I know I wouldn't make it. I'd either suffocate on my way or get burned alive when I got there. I have to turn back and find my way around, which I quickly realize isn't an option either. The wreckage is everywhere. There's no logic to where the fire has spread and where it hasn't.

I picture an airplane crashing into a building and imagine what that impact would do. The solid structure of the Pentagon would've torn it open like a can of tuna fish. And just like whenever I try to open a can of tuna fish, what's inside would've splashed out all over the place. Aside from the luggage and the passengers—which I can't think too much about right now—it would have spilled fuel.

I can still smell it, but the thing about fuel being everywhere in the air is that the air itself could ignite and explode. No wonder the wreckage looks so random. Jet fuel ignited randomly all over the place. Weirdly, the stairwell door to my right looks totally undamaged, even though the walls around it are bent and broken.

When I touch the door handle, it's warm but not scalding hot. I push it open carefully, staying kind of back, because I remember the movie *Backdraft* that my dad loves. When you open a door in a fire, you can give sudden oxygen to the flame and cause it to blow up in your face.

Nothing blows up in my face though. The stairwell looks clear. A light fixture has fallen and another is dangling, but otherwise I can go up if I want to.

I think through my tour with Sergeant Guinsler. I remember this stairwell. I can take it to the huge Army section, where there were endless rows of cubicles. I can pass by the librarian's office and then hopefully go down the set of stairs that will put me right by the entrance to my dad's section on the first floor—right by the Sensitive Compartmented Information Facility where he'd been having a meeting.

My heart leaps with hope. The SCIF is probably a pretty secure location. That's where lots of top-secret work is done and secret documents are held. Maybe it's even reinforced against bombs and things. The Pentagon is a military installation, after all, and it looks like a fortress. Why shouldn't parts of it be secured like a fortress? If they are, then maybe my dad and some of his colleagues are safe in the SCIF right now, waiting for the all-clear sign so they can evacuate.

I can show them the way. I can help them all get out, and maybe even get some of the secret documents to safety too. I can be a hero!

In the distance, I hear a voice on a megaphone: "Inbound hostile aircraft! Fifteen minutes to impact!"

My heart rate picks up. Fifteen minutes to find my dad and get out of here again. *I can do this*, I tell myself. *I have to.*

I start up the stairs two at a time, keeping my face covered because the air is still hot. But it's better here than it was in the hallway. When I reach the top, I plan to test the handle, making sure it's not too hot either. I don't want to go charging into a fire just because I've got heroic ideas in my head. I'm excited and scared and hopeful, not stupid. I have to stay careful if I want to save anyone.

Well, relatively careful. I'm still charging through a burning military headquarters that's under attack while nobody on earth knows where I am. That is, on its face, not at all careful.

At the top of the stairs though, the door isn't even there. It's hanging sideways off its hinges. There's no fire I can see on the other side, so I climb over it. Then I freeze.

I'm in Corridor Five on the second floor. I remember the librarian's office was somewhere near here, though this floor too doesn't look like I remember it. There are at least two more sets of stairs in this hall as I make my way toward the E-Ring, and huge fire doors that look like they've closed in that direction.

Also, the floor itself isn't level. Slabs of it have broken loose. I'll have to literally climb between sections of floor to get to the next stairwell.

It's smoky and hot here too, and I'm a little light-headed. I can't help but cough. I'm not going to be able to stay long. I remember the masks and the breathing equipment the firefighters have on and wish I had some. I'm sweating and I know it's not a safe temperature in here. I also know it's getting hotter. My heroic dreams from just seconds ago evaporate like the steam I see rising from the seams in the floor.

I'm standing right next to an office door that's cracked open, smoke dribbling out from the crack. I push it with my toe and have to leap back suddenly when the fire inside flares up. I scramble away from it on my hands and knees, scurrying down the hall toward the next set of stairs. I can't afford to be so careless. I have to assume the worst of every doorway.

I tell myself I'm moving fast enough to avoid the flames, but my brain catches up to what my eyes saw.

There were burned bodies in there, and they were definitely not alive.

I want to scream or go back for help. I want to run down the way I came from and race into the fresh air. But instead, I pause.

The building rumbles. It's loud, creaking, like a ship in a storm. It feels like a small earthquake passes through. The floor under me wiggles, then stops. I can feel it sloping just a little more than it had been a second before. Did another plane already hit somewhere in the Pentagon? Were they wrong about how long they had? Surely I would've heard a much bigger noise.

But if that wasn't another plane hitting, what was it? What could make the whole building shake?

"Oh no," I say aloud. I start to wonder if a building that looks as sturdy as the Pentagon can collapse.

I move again, faster this time, hustling for the other stairs to get down to where I think the Defense Intelligence Agency offices are. Or where they were.

The door to this stairwell is still attached, but the frame itself is tilted at an angle like a fun house door. The whole section of wall here is bent crooked. Right across from the stairwell there's a door to an office or a conference room or something. It too is bent weirdly, with a big crack up the middle like something slammed hard into it.

I'm about to push through the bent stairwell door when I hear a sharp crack. The door across from me bends and shudders, but holds. I stop. The sound comes again.

CRACK!

The door flexes, and I hear a grunt. A human grunt.

"Hello?" I shout, trying to make out what I'm seeing in the darkness of the hallway. I trace the flashlight over and notice there's now a gap between the door and the frame. "Hello?" I yell again, moving closer. My light catches on an eye peering out through the gap. It winces away from the brightness.

"We've got three people in here!" a woman's voice shouts from the other side of the door. "We're stuck and there's a lot of smoke! The ceiling's collapsed."

I hate to delay looking for my dad any further, but I can't just leave these people trapped either. So I cross to them. I pull at the door, though of course that doesn't work. I yank and kick, and that makes even less impact.

"I can't get it," I tell them.

"Can you get help?" a man asks.

"I can . . . um . . . I can try?" I stop. I don't tell them the building's been evacuated. That we're under attack. That the creaking sounds they're hearing might mean the whole place is gonna come down. I don't want to scare them. I'm already terrified myself. I don't want to leave these people, but I can't help them on my own.

I shine my light up and down that hallway. "HEY!" I yell as loud as I can. I'm squatting near the floor because the smoke is too thick. "ANYONE THERE? I NEED HELP! HELP!"

For a moment the only sounds are my breath and the coughing from the other side of the door. I fear these people are doomed—and I'm doomed too if I stay with them. But then I hear the sound of heavy boots, debris shifting, and I see light from down the hall.

"Someone there?" a man shouts. I answer by waving my light around.

A squad of four firefighters hustles along the corridor in my direction. When their lights land on me, they look surprised to find a kid standing in this hallway. I don't have time to explain, and I don't think they're interested in explanations right now. They immediately hack the door open with their axes, freeing the people inside.

At the same time, one of them shoves an oxygen mask over my nose and mouth. That's when I realize how short of breath I've been. It feels amazing to get a few fresh, clean breaths, but I hardly have enough of them before they take the mask back to share it with the people now stumbling from the room, a man and two women in business attire. Civilians, though they're so covered in soot and dust that that's about all I can tell.

Before I know what's happening, the firefighters are leading us to the stairwell I'd just come up.

"I can't go this way," I tell them.

"We have to evacuate now," one of them says, helping move the mask from one civilian back to me. We're taking turns breathing, and it's amazing how much stronger it makes me feel. I probably haven't had a clean breath in half an hour.

I stop and stand firm. It's hot here, too hot to stop moving, and the building is making a lot of unpleasant groaning noises. But I can't take another step. I won't.

"We don't even know if there *is* another plane," I argue. I know I shouldn't be arguing with the men who are here to save my life, but I'm not ready to abandon my dad.

"What plane?" one of the survivors from the office asks.

"No plane," the firefighter says. "That was a false alarm. But the building is unstable! We have to move!"

Instead of crawling over the broken stairwell door like I did, two of the firefighters heave it out of the wall and start helping people down. I know that way leads outside, or at least it did a few minutes ago. I also know that it doesn't lead me to my dad's office.

"I have to go down the other stairs," I tell the firefighter, feeling myself about to cry. I take off the breathing mask and press it back into his hands. "My dad's office is down there! He needs me!"

The firefighter clamps a hand on my shoulder even as I back away. "Listen, kid . . . What's your name?"

"Mikey," I tell him. "Mikey Cutler. My dad's name is Dave."

"Okay, Mikey"—the firefighter squats in front of me, puts the mask back on my face—"I'm Chad. And I promise we have other crews looking for your dad and everyone else. But he would not want you in here searching for him. He would want you safe."

"Dave Cutler?" one of the civilians says from the stairwell door, moving back toward me. "I know your dad. He's in IT, right?"

"Sort of," I say. "He works with computers, but—"

We all flinch at a loud popping sound and a shriek like metal twisting.

"Move it, people!" one of the lead firefighters says. He's nearly shoving everyone down the stairs ahead of him, yanking the woman who knows my dad off her feet and tossing her over his shoulder. Chad's grip on me tightens. He's about to scoop me up the same way, giving me no choice in the matter.

"I'm sorry," I say, jumping out of his reach. "My dad's all I've got. You all go, but I won't leave him!"

With that, I'm gone, running for the stairs, closer to the flames.

MIKEY: 10:09 A.M.

I don't hear Chad shout, but I do hear him chasing me. I'm quick, and smaller than he is, so I can move around the debris on the floor faster. I make it to the second stairwell just ahead of him.

I'm through the door and onto the landing, ducking low because there are dangling wires overhead. As Chad bursts through, I shout a warning to watch out.

It's cooler in these stairs, though not by much. Which is weird, because they're closer to the front of the building where the plane hit. Somehow, the fire's bigger and hotter toward the inside than the outside. I don't understand it, but I don't really need to. I just need to keep moving.

The building rumbles. I'm taking the steps two at a time, and Chad's right on my tail. It's hard to stay balanced. Everywhere is uneven and wet from the massive amounts of water the firefighters have been spraying since the moment they arrived on the scene.

I nearly fall down the stairs, but Chad catches me by the arm, which keeps me from getting impaled on a section of rebar jabbing out from a break in the wall.

"I told you to go!" I yell at him.

"This is literally my job, Mikey!" he says. He sounds kind of mad. I guess I would be too in his situation. "And you're gonna need my help."

The stair landing is covered in debris, broken bits of the building everywhere, though the door is intact. I touch it and it's hot, but Chad knows better and after he touches it, he slams it open. The fire's burning in this part of Corridor Five, but at random points on the walls and ceiling, and I can see we've got a clear path toward my dad's section. The huge wall that used to separate it from the hall is gone.

There are desks and screens and filing cabinets everywhere, along with steel bars and slabs of concrete. Flames burn at random spots like campfires. There are also mountains of burning debris, from floor to ceiling, and in places the smoke is so thick, I can't tell the difference between walls and air.

"Dad!" I yell. I don't know what else to do. The yelling doubles me over, makes me cough. Chad shoves the breathing mask over my mouth again.

"Mikey, we can't stay here," he says, and he's pulling me down toward the floor and dragging me back toward A-E Drive.

"But—" I try to object.

"No one's there," he says. "No one alive."

"I can't leave him!" I cry. "Without him, they'll put me in foster care!"

He hesitates. Even under his mask, I see his face twitch. But then he shakes it away, pulls me back. "You'll be alive. It's not the end of the world."

He's fully dragging me now, and I don't have the strength to resist. Then there's a sudden cracking sound and a whoosh of air from the direction of E-Ring.

It all happens fast then.

Chad says a word I know I shouldn't repeat, and shoves me against the nearest corridor wall, down into a puddle of filthy water. Then he dives his body on top of me, covering me with his back and his fire-proof firefighter's coat. I've still got the breathing mask on and haven't dropped the flashlight yet, which is good, because all light vanishes with the loudest sound I've ever heard in my life.

The floor shakes, and I lose my footing. A wave of dust and debris crashes down the hall and then over us. I feel my body leave the ground with the force of the shock wave, though Chad never lets go of me.

My ear is by his radio and I hear voices squawking. "We have a pancake collapse. E-Ring. E-Ring collapse."

Everything is dark now. I'm pinned below Chad, and I think he's pinned by something else. I'm lying facedown. I want to turn my head or sit up, but I can't move.

"Chad?" I say, though my voice is weak. "Chad!" I try again, firmer.

He doesn't answer. I don't know if he's unconscious or just can't hear me. I hear the loud sound of his respirator, so I know he's breathing. My own mask is attached to his tank, so we're sharing air. How long can one of those little tanks last? My shouting and straining probably don't help, so I try to calm myself, to breathe slowly. There's literally nothing else for me to do.

I can't save my dad. I can't save Sergeant Guinsler. I put Chad in danger by running this way, and now I can't save him either *and* stopped him from saving me.

Nice job, Mike, I scold myself. *You've done it again.*

In the dark, unable to move, I remember the last time I made a series of dumb decisions that hurt someone. I remember my mom. It turns out I'm reckless, just like her.

It was a great day, one of those perfect fall days when the air is crisp and everything smells like possibility. You just know Halloween is right around the corner with all its candy and pranks. We *loved* Halloween. We would always do these group family costumes, like Mom and Dad as the two robbers in *Home Alone* and me as Kevin. After their divorce, Mom and I did pairs costumes: Captain Hook and Peter Pan, Flounder and the Little Mermaid. That year I wanted to do *Men in Black*, from the Will Smith and Tommy Lee Jones alien-hunting movie. I was excited about it because I thought we'd look cool in black suits and sunglasses.

I didn't know we wouldn't even be together by Halloween, thanks to me.

We were at a fall carnival that Saturday. It was kind of cool, like a miniature state fair with rides and games and cotton candy and stuff. Mom told me to stay near this one game where she knew the carny, who'd keep an eye on me. It was the game where you throw a Ping-Pong ball into a bottle and if it lands on the top of one without bouncing off, you win a fish.

It was boring and rigged, and I didn't want a fish in the first place.

So I wandered off to check out the fun house. I loved not knowing what I'd see around the next corner, how the walls bent and twisted, how nothing inside was as it seemed. I was only ten at the time, and I guess a ten-year-old wandering around alone doesn't look good. A cop found me, asked where my adult was, where I was *supposed* to be. When he hauled me back to the carny who said he'd watch me, the guy ratted out my mom almost immediately.

The police found her in a trailer with a lot of drugs. They say she was selling them, and she was definitely using them. She went to the hospital and then to jail, and because she had a record, I went to a temporary foster home. Then it was court and off to live with my dad.

All because I hadn't listened and stayed where I should have. I had just wanted to see the fun house.

Some fun I'm having now. I don't think I ever want to be in a fun house again.

"Mikey?" Chad's voice sounds strained. It cuts through my memories.

"Yeah?" My voice is strained too.

"Are you hurt?"

"I don't think so," I tell him. "You?"

It takes him a while to answer. "A piece of wall fell over on us. I can't move it and I can't move out from under it. My legs might be broken. Tough as you are, I don't think you can carry me. But if you try, you might be able to wriggle out from under me and get out of this spot."

"I can't leave you here," I say, nearly crying as I think about how I got him into this spot in the first place. I think about my mom, who I left behind, and my dad, who I may never see again. I've failed everyone just by not listening.

Chad lets out a wheezy little laugh. His voice is really muffled through the respirator he's wearing, but I can tell he's laughing. "I'm not saying *leave* me here, kiddo. I'm saying get outside and tell them where I am." He pauses. "Do you know where we are?"

"When that shock wave hit, we were in C-Ring, Corridor Five," I say, still proud of how well I remember the layout. Not that it matters anymore, but I could definitely get an A on my Pentagon report. "But what if the whole building collapsed on us?" I ask.

"We wouldn't be having this conversation," he says.

"Can you radio for help?" I ask.

"I can't reach it, but I don't hear any sound anyway," he tells me. "I don't think it's working anymore."

He's right. It's quiet. For a second, I fear that's because another attack took out the entire building and all the firefighters. I worry there was a nuclear attack and there's no more America, no more world at all, just mutant zombies wandering the wasteland. If I leave Chad here, maybe I'll become one of them too.

My imagination is running away from me again. I need to stay in the here and now, not in the there and then.

"Listen," Chad says, "it's hot on my back and I think there's gotta be a lot of fire out there. If we stay here, we will not survive. You need to focus now. Get out of this rubble and get help, okay? Can you do that?"

I take as deep a breath as I can. "I'll do it," I say. "I *will* get you help."

I think one more time about the guy stuck under the copier, about Sergeant Guinsler, about my dad. Those were people I didn't help today, but Lena and the baby? That skinny guy who worked with my dad? The people stuck in that upstairs office? I helped all of them. I guess that's what people have to do in a disaster—focus on who they *can* save, not who they can't. I can save Chad because I have to, and I have to save him because I can.

Only lift what you can carry.

"I got this," I tell him.

I start to wriggle out from under Chad. I can tell he's biting back a yell from how much it hurts to have me jostling him. Suddenly, the mask pulls on my face. I realize I have to leave it behind. He's gonna need the air, and anyway, the tank is on his back and there's no getting it off. If there was a way, he'd probably make me take it. I bet he'd say it's his job, though I doubt his job description tells him to jump onto me as a building collapses and protect me with his own body. That's not a job, that's a hero. I'm not gonna let this hero down.

"You *will* get out of here," I reassure him as I slip the mask off and wriggle free. "I promise."

It's a promise I really hope I can keep.

MIKEY: 10:20 A.M.

I crawl out from one pile of rubble into . . . more rubble.

The smoke is still thick and fires still burn, but now the mix of water and dust has created a hot sludge on everything, which makes it slippery to crawl. I slide on my belly until I find an open hallway and can get myself up to a crouch.

The fire doesn't seem to have reached this hallway. It's dark as a horror movie. I scan my flashlight over the walls and discover they're bent and bowed too. Where there were once sharp angles and straight lines, everything here is now curved and cracked, drooping from water damage or bent from the weight above. The path, however, does look clear.

I think I can go down this hallway and get to another of the huge arteries to the building, one that radiates out from the central courtyard to the exterior. If the way really is clear, I can get back to A-E Drive or anywhere else. Surely, I'll find help along the way.

I nearly break into a run, but my hopes are quickly dashed when my flashlight catches a giant puddle. Really, it's more like a lake, stretching from one side of the hallway to the other. On its surface is a glittering slick of fuel. Frayed and broken wires dance all around it. Live ones maybe. If one of them touches that water while I'm crossing it, I'll either be electrocuted or burned alive. For all I know, the water is already electrified.

There's no way around.

I have to go back. I have to try the other way, maybe see if I can take this hallway all the way to Corridor Four.

The thought turns my stomach. There's more smoke and fire and wreckage in that direction. That's also the direction of my dad's office. If I go that way, there's a chance I'll see that something horrible happened to him. Of course, if I go that way and don't even look for him, I'll feel terrible too.

I stand there for a moment with the weight of that, but I know Chad doesn't have the time for me to waste pondering my feelings. I made him a promise I have to keep.

I turn around and head toward the inferno, even though every cell in my body begs me not to. My back aches from so much crouching and bending and squishing under things, but I keep going. One foot in front of the other.

The hallway is filled with debris, and my light catches on a puddle of red. I gasp, fearing it's blood, but then I see the bundles of wet paper and tattered red folders. Some of them say TOP SECRET on them. I could probably read more if I stopped, but I don't have time. And as my dad always made clear about accessing classified information, it's a crime if you're not supposed to have it. Even in a disaster.

Then it occurs to me: These documents must have come from a SCIF, a Sensitive Compartmented Information Facility like the one where my dad's meeting was.

I swallow hard and choke back tears. If these secure files were blasted apart, then what must have happened to the people inside?

I try not to get caught up in those thoughts. I pick my way through, my flashlight scanning carefully so I don't run into anything dangerous.

It's hot where I'm crawling. There's steam too, and

drizzles of water pouring from the ceiling. Firefighters must be spraying right above me, beating back the flames. The air starts to get easier to breathe. I start to think I might just make it, when suddenly I see a ghastly face looming over me.

"Ahhh!" I scream.

"I think I'm stuck," the face says. I see that it's a person, a man, who has somehow been pinned by a column, halfway up a wall. "Can you help me?"

His head is literally jammed against a broken cubicle wall. The pillar and his legs aren't even touching the floor. He flinches in the beam of my flashlight, and his face looks a little purple from the pressure on his head. But it seems most of the pillar's weight is being held by the broken cubicle, so he wasn't crushed. His eyes are open and alert, though my light is currently blinding him.

I point the beam away and he gasps.

"You're a kid?" he says.

"I guess so," I tell him, although I don't feel like a kid anymore. Not after what I've seen.

"I know you," he says. "Dave's son?"

"Yeah!" My heart thunders. "You know my dad?"

"Yeah," the man says. "I know him. I was with him."

"Is he—? Did he—?" I don't know how to ask what I want to ask, because I'm afraid of what the answer will be.

"I don't know," the man says sadly. "One second, we were in our meeting discussing server room configurations in the Middle East. Then there was this noise, the loudest noise I ever heard, and the whole room exploded. I'm pretty sure I was blown off my feet. I woke up here, stuck." He swallows. His throat is dry. I should've brought drinking water with me.

"Let's get you down," I tell him. I work the cubicle under him loose, so he can slide down.

He lands hard on a heap of broken, wet tiles and slips, falling on his side with a hard *oof.*

"Can you walk?" I ask, trying to help him up, but he's a heavy guy and my arms are already exhausted.

"Yeah, I think so," he says. "Just numb. Gimme a second."

"We don't have a second," I snap, which startles him.

I'm wasting time. Chad is still trapped and my dad is still missing, and this guy is just sitting there. He's alive and he's not my dad and he's slowing me down. I want to scream. Why can't I find my dad? Why do I have to keep helping everyone but the one person I want to rescue? It's not fair!

"Okay," the man says, pushing himself up and coughing. His legs wobble a little but he stays upright. Now that I can see more clearly, he's pretty burned and bloodied. I feel bad for how angry I'd just been. None of this is his fault. None of it's mine either, I try to remind myself, but that's harder to believe. "I'm ready."

The man is tall and he looks strong. A military haircut, though he's in civilian clothes.

"Were you a soldier?" I ask him.

He smiles. "Rangers," he says.

That's when I get the idea. We can go back together to help Chad. With a former Army Ranger's help, I don't have to leave the firefighter behind at all.

"You ready for one more mission?" I ask.

He cocks his head at me, puzzled.

"There's a fireman back that way who needs us," I say.

"We gotta get out of here," the Ranger says, which is a refrain I've been hearing too much.

I shake my head. "We don't leave anyone behind," I tell him. I make sure the flashlight is showing my face so he knows I'm serious.

He shakes his head. "This is a job for professionals," he says. "First rule of search and rescue is you don't put more people in danger, especially civilians. It just makes it more dangerous work for the rescuers when they have to save you too."

"But he saved my life!" I object.

"Kid, I can't let you go back into the fires," he says. "And this firefighter wouldn't want you to either. You saved my life just now, and I gotta get you out of here. Your dad would never forgive me if I didn't."

His face looks just as set as mine. And worse, I know he's right.

But my dad's not here, and Chad is. I have to help him.

I do something I'm not proud of right then, something I know is wrong. But it's a split-second decision that I make.

I lie.

"Okay," I say. "I saw a way out back there." I turn to lead him along this hall back to Corridor Five, back to where Chad is. I mean, it's not a *total* lie, because there probably is a way out, somewhere. But if we find the firefighter before we get there, then we can help him too. For all I know, it's safer in this direction.

I lead the Ranger back down the hall, crouched below the smoke. He tears the sleeves off his suit jacket to wet them, the fine cloth making a better breathing mask than my shirt did.

We head toward the corridor where Chad is, and I try to ignore the voice in my head telling me this is wrong, that I should get us both out of here as quickly as possible and not put him or myself into any more danger. I should do what I told Chad I would: Get outside to send professionals back for him.

But I don't think there's time.

There are other voices in my head too. Voices telling me to keep looking for my dad and ditch this stranger altogether. Send help for Chad *after* I find my father.

There's also a voice telling me never to leave this disaster zone, to stay inside for as long as I can breathe, because the moment I go out, the moment I surrender to help from the grown-ups, is the moment the next part of my life starts. The part where my dad is dead and my mom's in jail and I get put into foster care for good.

Inside here, I'm fighting for survival. It's me versus the fires.

Outside, I'm just a lost kid.

Given that choice, I choose the fires.

I crawl forward, leading the way. When we reach a huge bent-up piece of scaffolding that must have shifted since the first time I came through, the Ranger—whose name I don't even know—moves forward to clear the way. He's strong and holds it so I can get through, then comes through himself.

We're nearly back at the hall where I left Chad when something above us cracks. Suddenly, a section of the ceiling slams down with a cloud of dust and splash of mud. The Ranger disappears behind it.

"You okay?" he shouts through the rubble.

"I'm okay!" I shout from the other side, rubbing my hands over my body just to make sure nothing has impaled me. "Can you get through?"

"Looks like a whole piece of the ceiling and the vents came down," he says. "I can't move it." I hear grunting. "We're cut off." He starts coughing. "Smoke's pretty thick over here."

"It's okay here," I say.

"I can't . . ." He coughs. "I can't stay here."

"Go!" I yell. "Go back the way you came. There's a way out behind you. A broken hole in the wall that goes to A-E Drive!"

"There's . . ." He coughs. "What?"

"A way out," I say. "I saw it before . . . I just . . . I wanted us to go this way . . ."

He's silent, and I don't think it's because he can't talk. It's just hitting him that I lied about the way out, that I was tricking him.

"I had to help Chad," I say, though it comes out like a plea, like an apology. I'm kind of begging this stranger for forgiveness.

I hear movement on the other side, metal shifting. He's trying to come through, but then he's coughing again. "Kid! I can't get through this! I can't . . . I'll send help . . ." Another coughing fit.

"Go!" I say, and when I don't hear a response, I hope that means he's turned back and not that's he passed out. I can see plumes of smoke coming through the rubble.

Please, I beg. *Please let him make it out. Please don't let me have led him to his death.*

"I'm sorry!" I shout, in case he can still hear me. I'm crying now. "I'm sorry!" I say again, wanting to collapse right there, just like the ceiling. But I have to get back to Chad. I turn and my heart sinks.

This way is blocked too.

Of course, the Ranger was right. This is why you shouldn't put yourself in more danger trying to rescue someone if you have no training. Not if you're a middle schooler, who's already hurt and scared and exhausted and doesn't really have any idea what he's doing. Not if you're reckless and impulsive. Not if you suffer from delusions of grandeur, imagining yourself a hero when you're just a fool. Not if you're me.

I lay back on the floor, staring at the small patch of hallway that's sealed me in, watching the smoke and dust dance in my flashlight beam. This time, I can't talk myself out of giving up. I can't talk myself into moving. I can't talk myself into anything at all. I'm trapped.

What have I done?

SAGE

I hear a word I know.

"Pancake," crackles over the radio and my ears prick up, but I don't smell pancakes. Normally, hearing "pancakes," I would smell the flour and the sugar and the vanilla and the eggs. Traces of dish soap from the bowl. Traces of tomato sauce on my human's favorite stirring spoon that they never clean quite as well as they think they have. Maple syrup.

Now, I smell only disaster.

Just as I hear that breakfast word and think about eating, a huge section of the large building crumbles down on itself. From my spot in the back of the truck, I can see it happen. The burning section of this large squat structure crumbles and collapses onto itself, one floor at a time. From the fifth floor all the way to the ground, like a slice taken out of a . . . well, out of a stack of pancakes.

Stranger still, is that some of the spaces I can now

see on either side of this collapsed wedge are almost intact. There is a human's desk with a globe beside it just sitting there on the edge of the open air. There's a big room with a long table, and though the room is tilted slightly, it's almost otherwise undisturbed.

I see these things, but I could not think of a way to describe them other than by what's there. Humans are clever like that, using a breakfast word to describe something that isn't breakfast at all.

Humans are good at poetic images. Us dogs, not so much.

The smells haven't changed, though the collapse blows some of them up into the air in bigger clouds. Fire and smoke smells are pushed away by the collapse, growing fainter. I wonder if the force of it blew out some of the fires.

That would be good. The sooner the fires are out, the sooner I can get to work in the rubble.

I like searching rubble. In training, I learned how to sniff for my handler and then bark when I found them. Pretty simple right?

Well, then they make that person *not* my handler, and I have to bark at *them*. Then that person is a total stranger and I have to bark at them on my handler's command. *Then* that person hides in a box, and I have to find them and bark at them. And *then*, guess what? There are empty boxes too, and boxes with other smells in them, like even delicious smells, and I have to pick the one where I smell the person I don't even know, and bark near it, and if I do all that? *Then* they have me do it again in actual rubble, where someone is hiding. Every time I signal and bark at the person I've found, I get to play the most epic game of tug-of-war with my handler.

It's a blast.

They don't reward me with treats during these games, because I guess they don't want me thinking I can just eat whatever smells good at a disaster. Which makes sense, but come on—I'm a dog! I know what I can eat and what I can't!

Except that one day, when I ate my handler's whole turkey-and-cheese sandwich off the dashboard of her truck.

And that other time I ate a bag of candy from the break room table and had to go to the vet.

And when I ate a sock and pooped string for a week.

Okay, I admit it, one thing dogs aren't great at is knowing when something is safe to eat or not. Whatever.

We can't be good at *everything*, and I'm good at so very, very much. I'm excited to get my chance to show off, to do my job, and then to PLAY!

I can smell how upset the people around me are. They could use a good play too. People don't admit it, but they love to play when I make my finds as much as I do. We're all so happy when I make a find. I can't help but wag my tail thinking about it.

There are so many people around, so many smells, this is going to be a tough one. But I bet I'll make so many finds my handler's arms are going to wear out from all the playing we'll do. I'm gonna save some human lives today, and I'm gonna have a great time doing it.

I see more fire trucks and ambulances zooming around. The firefighters are battling blazes all over the west side of the building. Jets of water cut lovely lines through the clear sky. Plumes of black smoke and white steam rise from the wreckage. A breeze passes over, shifting the smoke, rustling the trees. I notice a few trees near the giant hole in the side of the building are burned to cinders. It's a shame. I really like trees.

Thousands of people make their way across the

parking lot; they're carrying the injured; they're help-ing each other. I'm a trained professional rescuer, of course, but it looks like today everyone is a rescuer, in uniform or out. I start to wonder if I'll have anything to do, or if the people will have already rescued each other before I get the chance to find anyone.

A firefighter comes over to talk to my handler and the driver in the front seat, and he's looking grim and determined. Smells like smoke too, and sweat. I'm pretty sure he's come from inside the building. He's even got some blood on him, though I don't think it's his own.

There are two men with him, one in uniform, limp-ing, smelling of blood. He's injured. The other wears a tattered and burned suit. He's also injured. His arm is bound up in a kind of sling made from a piece of silk, the sort some humans wear like decorative collars. Neckties, they call them. He's using it to hold up his damaged arm.

I can smell the wounds on both men, and they're serious. Burns and cuts. Why are they here in the parking lot talking when they should be getting help from one of their human veterinarians?

Anxiousness oozes out of the man in the suit's pores

with a stronger stink than any of his other smells, which are pretty strong to begin with. He tells my handler, "I know my son is alive. Sergeant Guinsler here talked to him *after* the crash. He made it out, but—"

The man starts to cough. He's having trouble talking, though I can't tell if it's because he's badly hurt or badly upset. Humans are prone to all sorts of damage, and not all of it can be seen. Some of it can't even be smelled.

"When I got out, I asked on A-E Drive about him," the uniformed man, Guinsler, says. He smells strongly of smoke and sweat and blood, his own and other peoples'. I get the sense he's been helping, even though he's hurt himself. A rescue dog can recognize another helper, even when we're not the same species. He smells like a helper. Also, he smells faintly of cinnamon. Faded, not enough to make me sneeze or itch, but enough to make me point my nose away. It's not a smell I like at all.

"Someone said they saw Mikey go back inside," he continues. "He went *back* in. Maybe half an hour ago. Before the collapse."

"He went back for me," the other man weeps. "He's in there!"

"Sergeant, thank you," says the firefighter, letting the helper comfort the sad man.

I don't catch the rest of what they're saying, but they look at me and point. My tail wags. The uniformed man—Sergeant Guinsler, I think—reminds the sad man about something. The sad man unties the silk cloth from his arm, wincing all the while. He gives it to my handler. He's still crying. I hear the word "son" again.

I'm really listening now as my handler and the driver move to talk privately near the back of the truck, right by me.

"It's not policy," the driver says. "The scene isn't secure. The FBI will be angry. They've told me nine times already that this is an active crime scene."

"It's an active disaster," my handler says. "And Sage can help find this man's son."

"The fire is ongoing," the driver tells her. "You two go in there and it'll be extremely hazardous."

"If this were your son, would we be having this conversation?" my handler asks. She's already putting on protective equipment while she talks.

The driver doesn't answer her, but his body language tells me he's letting her go in. Which means he's letting *me* go in.

Which means I have a job to do!

My handler's got my favorite toy in her pack now and clips my leash on. I jump right down onto the pavement, and she squats in front of me to scratch behind my ears. She talks to me like a person, which I appreciate, even though I can't answer in her language.

"We're going in to look for a boy who's lost in there," she says. She puts the tie in front of me, lets me sniff it. There are the man's smells, and lots of smoke, but also it smells like a drawer in a boy's room. There's some sweat on it, some fabric softener, some hints of the things it must have shared the drawer with. There are boy's room smells, which are very distinct. Teenage human boys are like a stew of stink that I think other humans find gross, but are irresistible to a dog like me. My tail is already wagging. These smells are strong. I'm not the least bit worried about being able to find this kid.

My handler leads me toward the boy's dad. "What's his name?" she asks.

"Mikey," he says. "Mikey Cutler. Someone said they saw him in Corridor Five a little before the collapse."

My handler scratches behind my ears. "Then that's where we'll start."

She tries to put protective booties on my paws, but I hate how they feel and can't help wriggling away. I even nip at her hand, which I know is not appropriate—but I can't do my job if my paws aren't free.

"I know you hate these," she says. "But it's gonna be hot in that rubble and we need to protect your paw pads."

I let out a whine, but I allow her to put them on me. I can tell she feels good that I've obeyed her in front of all these people. I guess the discomfort is worth it if it makes her happy.

"Please," the father says. "Find my son."

"We'll do our best, sir," she tells the man, and we leave him, teary-eyed and soot covered, as she leads me across the huge parking lot toward the burning building.

We're escorted by two firefighters, one of whom I guess is like a pack leader. Because as he goes, he barks orders at other firefighters and they hop to it. It feels good to have such an important human escorting me to my work. Makes me feel important too.

Mikey, I think. *I'm coming to find you, Mikey, wherever you are. Just stay stinky and you'll be okay.*

I wish I could shout that out, but I don't have the

words and it's too loud here anyway. I could bark, I guess, but I know better. I won't bark until I find the boy.

When I do, I'll bark so loud, every dog for miles will know that Sage has saved the day.

MIKEY: 10:25 A.M.

I'm alone. Deeply, completely alone.

I shout for help a few times, but the shouting hurts my raw throat and it's just too hard to do. I'm having trouble getting enough air, even through the sleeve I'm using as a mask.

There are puddles here in my small patch of hall-way. I know it's gross, because they're filthy and filled with all kinds of terrible chemicals, but I sip some of the dirty water from the floor. I try to use the sleeve as a filter for it, but it's still chunky and disgusting. It does help my throat though. Makes me feel a tiny bit better. Right now, "a tiny bit better" is a huge victory.

I'll probably throw up later, but that's a worry for later . . . if I survive.

I shine the beam of my flashlight around. Behind me, the collapsed part of the ceiling is impenetrable and blazing hot. Most of the smoke and flame are venting upward through the hole the collapse created, which must be how I'm alive.

On the other side of me, on the way back toward Corridor Five, I realize that what at first looked like a solid wall of twisted metal is actually a mix of broken concrete, drywall, metal, and plywood. It's the construction scaffolding from the work they were doing to renovate this section.

Despair turns to hope as I crawl over to it. The plywood is probably pretty weak from all the water and fire. If I can kick through a piece, I might be able to crawl through the rubble. I might make it out of here and back to Chad! I might still save him and myself too!

I've never been good at wallowing. I like action. Maybe it's what gets me into trouble, but I just can't sit still. Doing *something* makes me feel like myself again.

I find a spot that looks especially flimsy and work my way to it feetfirst on my back, so I have leverage for kicking. I can't stand up, but I'll need to stay low anyway—out of the smoke. Better to crawl than to climb.

In order to reach the section of plywood, I have to really shimmy into the heap, wedged in right below some jagged pieces of aluminum tubing and a chunk of cinderblock that's pinned the whole thing in place. Hopefully, kicking myself free won't topple the whole tower. It's right above my head, just a few inches away. If the barricade does come down, it'll decapitate me instantly.

At least it won't hurt for long, I tell myself as I pull back my leg and prepare the first kick.

I wonder if I should pray. I've never been religious, but I figure it couldn't hurt. Right now, I need all the help I can get.

"Dear God," I say, like I'm writing Him a letter. But talking makes me cough and it's just too hard. I'm sure He'll understand if I just think my prayer. Also, I don't even know if He is a He or, like, something else. She or They or some other word humans don't even have. I mean, if there is a God, isn't it a God of all living things, like ducks, bacteria, and dogs? Not just creatures who look and think like people do?

Dear God, I start again in my head. *It's Mikey Cutler, in case You don't know. I . . . um . . . I could use Your help, I think. I'm sorry I don't pray more. Or, like, ever. I hope that doesn't upset You too much. I've had a lot going on with my mom and stuff and I guess . . .*

I swallow hard, staring at the circle of light my flashlight is making in the bent wreck of metal above me, the strange shadows it casts that look a lot like prison bars.

I guess I was angry about my mom. I guess I still am. It's not fair. None of this is fair. And I can't believe You'd let any of this happen.

I think about all the people I saw on A-E Drive, people with burns and broken bones and worse. I think about the people who didn't make it, the bodies right now all over this building who just came to work today and will never get to go home again. The people in the Twin Towers in New York too. And the people all over the world who die every day, and wonder how any sort of God could let all this bad stuff happen. If there really is a God, then none of it should.

My fists are clenched, my body shaking with anger.

You know what? I think at God. *Never mind. I'll do this myself.*

And then I kick the wood, hard. It makes a loud cracking sound but holds.

I don't need You, You hear me! I shout in my mind,

my rage boiling even hotter than the flames. I kick again.

CRACK!

It bends. I hear metal shift, but nothing falls. I kick again.

CRACK!

There's an opening! I feel my anger leaving me as I wiggle forward to push the plank with both legs, bending it away, making a hole. I might be able to crawl through!

I have to scooch back out of my little nook to turn my face forward with my flashlight and crawl again. I can see through the hole I've kicked open and, sure enough, there's a path out of the debris, almost like a tunnel. It's not straight and there's jagged metal going this way and that, but I can make it.

I'm not sure I would've found the strength to kick through that plank if I hadn't been so angry. If *praying* hadn't made me so angry.

I wonder if that's the answer right there. The anger is what I needed. Maybe God's not like a video game, where you punch in the right keys in the right order and you get a cheat code for life. Prayer isn't cheat code.

Maybe God is more of a question. Can you do more than you ever thought possible? Can you find what you need where you are and share it, even when it might not be enough? Can you endure the terrible things of the world and not lose yourself?

There's no bearded guy in the sky who made my mom a drug addict, or crashed planes into buildings, or made me go back inside to find my dad. Those were human choices. We keep doing our best and doing our worst—and getting it all mixed up. Maybe God is the best way we can describe finding the strength to keep crawling through it, even when we're hurt.

I laugh at myself in the dark, because I'm thinking all these super-deep thoughts, but I'm up to my elbows in sludge.

It looks like there were cans of paint or primer or something that burst open and splattered everywhere, mixed with the water from the fire hoses. Together, they created a seriously slick mess. I can't help slipping, moving slower than I'd like. The space is getting tighter and it's hard not to think about the tons of wreckage above me that could come crashing down any second. I have to speed up.

When I try to use my knee to shove forward, it slips

on a broken tile. I feel the jagged edge of something slice my shin.

"AHH!" I yell. I try to curl up to grab it, to see if it's bleeding, but there's not enough room.

I drop the flashlight, which tumbles between broken pieces of a pipe. I try to reach down to pick it up, but I can't quite get to it. It casts strange shadows all around me, like I'm in a metal thornbush in some kind of demented sci-fi fairy tale.

I stretch toward the light, straining, and hear fabric tear. Part of my shirt is caught. I can't free my arm. I try to yank my hand back, but I'm stuck. I'm lying on my belly on an uneven mess of wood and metal, and I can't even turn my head fully to see *where* I'm stuck. I shake and pull to try to rip the shirt free, my shin stinging terribly the whole time. I kick a little too, hoping that will help.

The kick is a mistake.

I hear a rattling and a scraping of metal against metal. A creak.

I freeze, but the pile doesn't.

The scaffolding above me shifts with a roar like an eighteen-wheeler's brakes. The plywood I'd kicked open to crawl through suddenly folds as a giant piece of the structure smashes down onto it, closing off the route back. The jaws of metal in front of me—my way out—snap shut too.

I squeeze my eyes closed as well, expecting all the broken, sizzling, jagged shrapnel above to crush me into hot pudding. It doesn't. Instead, it settles. I'm in the belly of a wrecked metal beast, but I'm still alive.

For now.

Except I'm deep under this rubble, lying on my stomach with sharp things digging into me all over. I'm bleeding from my shin, struggling to breathe through a suit sleeve, and I'm well and truly unable to move.

And that's when the flashlight conks out, plunging me into a darkness more total than anything I've ever known.

Dear God, I'm in trouble now, I pray again, not because I think I'll get a different answer than before, or even because I've suddenly become a believer in my literal darkest moment. I pray because there's nothing else to do. I'm alone, and a prayer going up and out—or even just through my head—makes me feel a little less alone.

And there's a tiny part of me that hopes—defying all logic, even though I'm only thinking it—that somebody, somewhere, might hear me.

SAGE

We approach the entry doors from the parking lot, but a team of firefighters waves us back, and not even the authority of the pack leader with us—a man they call Captain—can get us through.

"It's burning over a thousand degrees this way," one firefighter says. "No one is alive in this section."

Emphasizing the point, I see a group of firefighters exiting at that moment, looking exhausted, their thick fireproof coats steaming. They've come to change air tanks and give another crew a shot at the hoses.

My small team of humans regroups and comes up with a new plan. We have to get back in our vehicles and drive around the building, into a tunnel, and come out in the courtyard, where we can make our entrance at the last place this boy, Mikey, was seen.

So it's back in the car I go, though this time the Captain's pickup truck leads us, sirens blazing. We go so fast I have to lie down. I can't even sit up to look out the window like I usually do. It upsets my tummy a little bit if I'm being honest. And an upset tummy is one of my least favorite things. It starts to make me feel nervous, and then I feel even more nervous when we go through the tunnel underneath the big building.

There are hoses and firefighters all around, and ambulances screeching by even faster than us. Our headlights blaze forward through dust and smog. I don't like it in here, and I'm relieved when we come out into what looks like a park.

I wonder why this big building has a park right in the middle of it. I want to pop my head up to see it better, but we're still moving fast, weaving through. When I try to sit up, I can't get my paws stable in the booties, so I skitter and scrape and thump onto my side. It's embarrassing. I'm not some clumsy, nervous puppy.

I decide to stay lying down until we come to a stop a few minutes later. We're in a narrow drive, almost like a street between buildings. I'm not sure how we got here, but the air smells so strongly of fire and destruction that I know we must be close to the disaster itself.

My handler lets me out, clipping my leash again, and we make our way to where the Captain is talking to some other firefighters. They're pointing at big openings in the wall, broken spots that don't look like doors. They look like holes I might dig to bury a bone. They're surrounded by heaps of rubble. I even see a huge burned wheel that smells like jet fuel.

This must be the place. The Captain is telling my handler where to go in.

"The boy was last seen through this door, heading up Corridor Five," the Captain says. "But we've got reports of flare-ups, structural weakness, and col-lapses. There's a team in there now putting out some of the flames. If you stick behind them, you should be okay for a bit. It's not a good idea, but—"

"But there could be a kid alive in there," my handler says, all the fear gone from her voice. Her shoulders are back, her chin up. She's all confidence. Her body language makes me feel confident too, and I perk up, ready. I'm not even panting anymore. I'm in work mode. Once you get a dog like me in work mode, we don't stop until we get the job done (and get our reward, of course).

She leads me past the big holes in the wall, to the

door. It takes me a bit to get comfortable walking in my weird booties, but I'm glad I have them on, because the ground is hot and covered in all kinds of sharp junk. It's dim and smoky and even with my handler's light and the work lights the firefighters have set up, it's hard to see much of anything.

Luckily, seeing isn't the most important thing for me right now. Sure, I need to see. Dogs can't rely *only* on their noses. But my nose is what's gonna tell me where to go. My eyes and ears and paws are what'll get me to where my nose points.

I'm so excited to get started, I pull the leash.

"Heel," my handler orders, calming me. I return to her heel, walking at her side and sniffing.

"There's a collapse ahead!" a firefighter yells through his mask, which muffles his voice. "Hallways branching here and here."

He's pointing side to side, and my nose works the air. I sniff for any trace of the scents I picked up on the necktie, any trace of live human beings at all. There are so many different smells rushing at me. I'm almost dizzy, and for a moment I fear I'm not up to this. I'll never figure out what's what or where it's coming from. My whole body is tense as I sniff, but so far, I get nothing useful.

Until I catch something. It's sweat and blood and breath. It's faint, but it's alive and it's coming from somewhere straight ahead in the big hallway. I pull again, nose forward, tail straight.

My handler resists, pulling me back.

Ugh! I remember she's not my usual handler. Maybe she doesn't know all my body language or understand what I'm trying to tell her. *That way!* I'm saying. *I smell something that way!*

In frustration, I bark.

The firefighters startle, but to her credit, my handler stays cool. She bends down, well below the smoke line that lingers up at human head height. She unclips my leash. "Go, find," she says, and I'm off, racing ahead. She keeps her light shining on me, so she doesn't lose me in the dark.

I'm at the huge pile of rubble in a flash, and my nose gets to work, weaving over the edges, then picking my way carefully up the heap. It's slick with water from the firefighters' hoses, but I don't feel any live fires. I keep climbing, checking each piece of rubble, looking for clues.

I have to weave back and forth over the rubble, treading lightly so I don't stumble. Then I lose the scent and turn back, heading toward the wall. For a moment, I think I've lost it for good, then it comes back to me, a trace of live human smell again. It's male, and it's ripe, and that makes me excited that I'm on track. I move back down to a gap in the rubble where it's strongest, and I start pawing at it. Every swipe of my paw brings more of the scent my way.

Yep, there is definitely something down there.

I stop pawing and let loose my loudest alert bark. And then another, and another.

The humans come running.

My handler whistles me over and immediately rubs my head. She tells me what a good boy I am, then gives me my toy for a nice game of tug. Meanwhile, the firefighters shift and dig through the heap until they find a section of fallen wall. It takes four of them to heave it up.

Even from a few feet away where I'm playing tug, I smell the burst of scents as the wall comes up. They uncover the human being lying there, alive.

I even stop my favorite game to look, just to see the amazing work I've done.

Except it's not a boy.

It's a firefighter—injured, barely awake, but alive.

The others hoist him up, radio for a medic, and immediately start carrying him out of the smoky corridor.

"It's Chad," one of them says. "Chad, can you hear me, buddy?"

The firefighter answers weakly. "A boy, Mikey, about thirteen years old. He make it?"

"We're still looking for him," my handler tells the injured firefighter as he's carried past. The firefighter gives a weak thumbs-up. I can smell the rise of hope in him, and that's how I know we're going to keep searching as disappointed as I am.

I let go of the toy without even being told to and my handler puts it back in her bag.

I'm afraid I don't know how to do this, that I don't even know where to start. But I'm not about to give up. I stick my nose to the ground and start sniffing, weaving back and forth down the corridor, poking my nose wherever my handler points.

All I've got so far is fire and fuel and the smells of death and decay.

Nothing living, nothing alive.

My nose and paws have already started to hurt from the smoke and heat, and I don't know how much lon-ger I can do this. But somewhere there's a kid who's counting on me, and no dog in history has ever wanted to let a kid down.

I don't intend to either.

MIKEY: 10:35 A.M.

I must've fallen asleep, although asleep or awake doesn't really matter in this darkness. My whole body hurts, which I guess is how I know I'm still alive. It's really hard to breathe now. I don't think I have any sweat left in my body. I still can't see anything, and I can't even hear anything either. It hurts to open my eyes, so I close them again, trying to just breathe and not think too much about how terrible I feel.

In the history of thinking, telling yourself not to think has never, ever worked.

I'm thinking even more now.

Lying in the dark, trapped below who knows how much rubble inside a military headquarters that's maybe about to collapse, all I can do is think.

I think about my mom, trapped in a different sort of government building. Trapped there by her sickness, her circumstances, and her choices.

I think about my choices, how they've trapped me here.

I think about my dad, hoping he's still alive, wondering if he's searching for me, if he's grieving me, or if he's past all that, lying dead in the rubble somewhere himself.

I can feel tears streaming down my cheeks, which is another way I know I'm alive. I'm glad for the sadness though. I'm glad to feel anything other than pain and fear. The sadness is a gift. It's my body and my heart telling me that even in my thirteen years alive, I loved people and they loved me. Even if this is the end for me, I'll know that I was loved. That's a lucky thing.

In the darkness, crying, I laugh.

I'm lucky, am I? I think, laughing harder. Maybe that's the proof of God I've been looking for. Even buried alive below burning rubble, I can find a reason to feel lucky. That's about as much of a miracle as I can imagine.

Laughing makes my throat and mouth hurt. I can feel that my teeth and tongue are filled with grit. I'd love to wash them out, but I've got no water, and I can't even reach the puddles of filthy muck now, stuck as I am.

I can reach my pocket though, and I remember the gum Sergeant Guinsler gave me. I don't even like cinnamon, but chewing gum will produce saliva, and that might be just what I need for my mouth to feel a little better.

It takes what feels like an hour, though it's maybe just a minute or two, to work the pack of gum out of my pocket, wriggle it to my face, unwrap it with one free hand, and pop it into my mouth.

It's delicious.

I've been tasting nothing but smoke and dust and jet fuel for an hour at least. Now my mouth is bursting with the fresh, spicy sweetness of cinnamon gum. I'm not sure I've ever tasted anything so good. With every chew, my mouth explodes in pleasure. This is joy. This is pure, simple joy.

This is great, I think as I chew what might be my last piece of gum ever. The air is so thick, it's making my brain kind of foggy. I'm not getting enough oxygen and my heart starts to race, which doesn't help. My ears are ringing and I feel like I'm going to pass out.

Part of me knows that if I pass out, I won't ever wake up.

But I'm not ready to die, not quite yet.

I really want to finish this gum.

That's all I can think about, just to keep chewing.

I chew and chew like that's what I'm born to do, like this is the best gum I've ever tasted in my life.

I picture Lena and her baby, safely on their way to the hospital to get checked out. The guy my dad worked with, getting treatment.

All I can do is chew, so I chew. I love cinnamon now. I love having lived in a world where cinnamon exists. I chew more.

I think about the people from that second-floor office, going home tonight with a story to tell. I see the Army Ranger stepping out into the sunlight, no sleeves on his suit, blinking, and taking a deep, clear breath. I even picture Chad, and somehow I just know he'll be okay. He has to be. I *feel* it.

I chew.

I picture my mom and my dad, both alive, both smiling at me. Even the sadness in their eyes is beautiful. They're alive, and they love me. They *loved* me, each in their way. I loved them too. I still do.

So I chew.

I can feel the fog in my brain thickening. I keep chewing, but I know I'm drifting away. That's okay.

I'm so tired. I could use a rest, but I just keep chewing. Lucky or unlucky doesn't matter anymore. I feel calm. Comfortable. *I'm a lucky kid*, I think, holding that image of my parents in my head as long as I can, tasting the cinnamon as deeply as I can. It's probably the last thing I'll ever taste. It's pretty good. *I'm such a lucky kid.*

SAGE

"Blockage down this hall, and the fire above's taken out the supports," a firefighter tells my handler. "You can't go down there."

"Sage is a live-find dog," my handler explains. "There's a child somewhere in here, and Sage is trained to locate him. He's the best chance we have of bringing that boy out alive, and he has found a scent!"

The firefighter looks at me and I look back at him. I'm focused, sniffing, and alert. I'm still searching.

But I haven't found a scent.

Another thing to know about dogs is that we don't lie. At least, not on purpose. When we do something wrong, we're ashamed of it. We get caught, we tuck our tails. But we don't pretend like nothing's happened. It's not a thing we'd even think to do.

But my handler has just lied.

There's a different signal she has to give me if she wants me to find a cadaver smell. I could find one of those easy right now. If that's the game we're playing, she needs to tell me. I'm a little frustrated, and I miss my usual handler. She'd never change the game on me like this.

Except, I know that she hasn't changed the game on me. I can feel her eagerness, her worry for this boy. She wants, more than anything, to bring him out safely, which she *can't* do if I'm not allowed to search. *That's* why she's lied. To keep looking. To help.

So I look at the firefighter and I sit.

One thing I hear humans say about a border collie's eyes is how "intelligent and soulful" they look. In the dim light of this smoky, sooty, sludgy, burned-out hallway, I try to give him my most intelligent and soulful look.

That's something else dogs know about humans: We know how to get what we want from them. We wouldn't have been humanity's best companions for thousands of years if we didn't.

"Fine," the firefighter relents. My eyes have done the trick!

He tells three of his guys to go with us down the hall. "But if they say fall back, you fall back—with the dog, with the kid . . . or without them. Got it?"

"Got it," says my handler. She points me toward the crossing hallway, then bends to whisper in my ear with a pat and a scratch. *"Good boy."*

This hallway is worse than the one we came from. It's hotter here, and there's more wreckage on the floor. The smoke is still pretty thick up high, and I can see my handler squatting and struggling a bit, even though she has a breathing mask on.

I don't have a breathing mask, and it does not feel good to breathe. It doesn't feel good to walk either, even with the booties on. The ground is hot and sharp and unstable. My handler is about to unclip me again so I can run forward and search, but one of the firefighters stops her.

He steps forward and puts a gloved hand on a charred piece of the wall. Then he steps back and uses a metal bar to poke at the spot he touched. When he does, the metal goes right through, opening a hole. A moment later, orange and blue flames burst out, like he just tore open a volcano.

I yelp and he leaps back and calls for a hose, which takes a while to arrive. A team of firefighters beat back the flames with torrents of water and swings from their axes. Then, after an eternity, all that remains is smoke and steam and even more mess in the hallway. But they signal to my handler that I can proceed. I don't know how much time I've lost, but it's even harder to pick up any human smells in this hallway, other than theirs.

Every spot on the wall looks like danger now and smells like fire. *Are more flames going to leap out at me?*

I hesitate.

I'm afraid. The fire erupting from the wall startled me, and dogs *do not* like being startled. At least, I don't.

It's not on purpose, but my tail tucks between my legs like it knows things I don't, things I don't want to know. Instinct, humans call it. Dogs don't have a word for it; it's just another way of *knowing.*

I shift from paw to paw but I don't move forward into the dark. I don't smell anything useful up ahead, just fire and ruin and death. I don't want to go there. I don't want to singe my fur or burn my paws raw. I'm too scared.

I'm not supposed to get scared.

I'm scared, which means I have failed.

I'm not the dog I thought I was.

I'm the not the dog they trained me to be.

I'm not the dog that boy needs.

I'm a failure.

I lie on the ground, in the wet rubble. A whimper slips out of me, shameful. I'm glad no other dogs are around to hear it. The handler squats next to me. I lean my body toward her, pressing my weight against the solidity of her legs.

"What is it, boy?" She rubs my ears, pats my side, feels along my body for injuries, though I'm not injured. At least, not in a way she can feel. Maybe dogs and humans aren't so different. Dogs can get hurt on the inside too.

She's not my usual handler, and she misreads my fear as knowledge.

"You getting something?" she asks.

I look at her, not trying to say anything with my eyes, but she can't help read the expression in them. Sometimes a dog can't help but make himself understood.

"You *afraid* of something?" She points. "Up there?"

There's a huge blockage up ahead, a heap of twisted metal and wood. Even as we squat there in the hall-way, it's smoking and steaming and we hear a clang. It shudders. It shifts. I retreat between my handler's legs.

I know it's going to collapse, just like I knew when part of the building would.

I sniff the air. There is a scent I don't like; it makes me sneeze. It's strong, and I can't stop sneezing. I feel my handler's worry rise.

"We need to fall back," the firefighter nearest us announces. "Fire's compromised that whole area. Construction scaffolding. Not meant to bear the kind of weight it's holding. It'll come down any second."

I sneeze again. The shifting scaffolding must have shaken something awful loose. I can't stop sneezing.

My handler pats me, clips my leash, and stands, leading us back toward the relative safety of the bigger corridor we came from. Pointing in the other direction, my sneezing stops. The bad smell must have been coming from that way, and I'm glad to get away from it. The memory of it is familiar but unpleasant.

As we walk carefully through the wreckage in the dark hall, my handler doesn't take my toy out of her bag. I don't get to play. I don't deserve to. I didn't find the boy. Maybe it's too late to find him anyway. Maybe another dog will find him, a cadaver dog, searching for the dead.

It's hot where I'm walking, but I suddenly feel cool,

like a cold mist. The firefighters up ahead are spraying up near the ceiling with their hoses and the steam drifts our way.

But that's not really what I'm feeling. The mist I feel is like a highland fog, something from a long time ago, an ancestor's fog. I feel the damp on my fur. I feel rocks and the moss under my feet.

And suddenly I'm not in this burning hallway anymore. I'm in the past with a border collie just like me—I'm connected to this ancestor-dog, seeing her across time itself.

Yeah, it's weird. I'm confused, but I watch and wait. The dog has something to teach me. She's circling a cliffside, rounding up the sheep in her flock because there's danger about. Wolves prowling the hills.

And she hears a bleating. I hear it too, because in this memory, I'm inside her fur, feeling what she feels, knowing what she knows.

She scents a pack of wolves on the wind, and stops, sniffs. Shudders.

She is afraid.

And there, alone on the edge on the hillside, separated from his flock, is a lamb, a young sheep who's gotten lost. Instinct tells her the wolves are closing in.

Instinct tells her she is outnumbered. Instinct tells her to keep the rest of the flock safe and let the little lamb perish. Some lambs cannot be saved.

But she's trained to protect the flock.

She has been bred to protect the flock.

The lamb is part of the flock, and what kind of dog would she be if she didn't try?

She charges, barking, weaving through the grown sheep, and racing up the hill. She leaps from rock to rock until she has reached the lonely lamb.

It bleats, afraid, and the wolves reveal themselves, teeth bared.

She barks, she snarls, she shows them her own teeth. And more than that, she shows them her*self*. The wolves can see she is not afraid.

She's outmatched, but she is fearsome. If they mean to take this lamb from her, it will cost them.

They back down and she leads the lamb to safety, like a border collie does.

I feel it all happen in an instant, and I know there is no difference between me and her. In the moment a lost lamb needs to be saved, all dogs are the same dog, all time is the same time. I am myself and I am my ancestors, bred into me. Her brave heart beats in my chest, and I know everything she knew. We are one. We are the same. We are rescue dogs.

And we are needed.

I turn back toward the dark.

I sniff and I sneeze—and I know the unpleasant smell.

It's cinnamon. The same smell that that uniformed man carried in his pocket but much stronger.

I pull toward it.

My handler pulls me the other way.

I sniff and sniff and try to sort the smells. The cinnamon, the smoke, the blood, but also . . . yes . . . human smells. *Live* human smells! And some of them I know. Some of them are the same as on that silk tie. And laid over it all, like a sign pointing the way, stronger and stronger, is that cinnamon stink.

I pull harder and the handler pulls back.

"We have to go!" she says. I ignore her, because I've got a scent, and when a dog like me finds its target, there's no calling us off.

I sniff. I lock in on the direction and point my whole body rigid.

I sneeze once, because I can't help it, and then, very much on purpose, I bark.

That's the signal.

I bark again.

My handler stops pulling. She knows it too.

I bark a third time.

"Wait!" she calls to the firefighters.

"We're falling back!" they shout.

"He's found someone!" I echo her with a fury of barking. She unclips me fast.

I know it's dangerous, but I run into the dark, barking. The firefighters hesitate.

"That's the signal!" my handler yells.

She follows me, and first one, then the rest of the firefighters fall behind us. They can't help it. Some humans can't let a lamb get lost either.

They follow me into the burning dark, every one of them.

I bark, and I sniff, seeking the scent, using it like a leash to lead me to the spot in the rubble where the smell is strongest.

I bark to tell the humans where to dig.

I bark to tell this boy I'm coming.

I bark and the fire burns and maybe the ceiling's coming down soon, but I bark and I bark and I bark. And somewhere, faint in the ruins, a voice replies.

"I'm here!" it calls. The voice smells like cinnamon. "I'm here!"

The boy's voice shouts, and then coughs, alive.

I bark.

He's here.

I bark.

Soon I'll get to play, because I've found him.

He's alive.

My bark pierces the thick air, echoes off the bent and broken walls.

I bark, because he's alive.

I bark and I bark and I bark.

Alive, I'm shouting in a language older than words. A language as old as dogs and humans working together. *Alive! Alive! Alive!*

MIKEY & SAGE: 11:00 A.M.

My dad is holding me and I'm breathing through a mask.

I'm not quite sure what's happened, but I'm in the sunlight, sitting on the back of an ambulance in a huge parking lot. I'm wrapped in a blanket, breathing the most amazing air of my life. The sky above is bright blue, clear, with a yellow late-morning sun warming my face. I squint at its brightness.

Faintly, I hear sirens and helicopters, but from where I'm sitting on the back of an ambulance, there is calm. My dad's one-armed hug feels safe and warm. I'm not sure how long he's been holding me. It feels like forever.

There's a woman with a black-and-white dog in front of us. She's standing, wearing a shirt that says FEMA on it, and the dog is sitting at her heel. Its eyes are almond shaped; they look kind and smart. My memory is a blur, but the dog looks familiar. A border collie.

While the paramedics check me over, I glance from my battered-looking dad to the kind-eyed dog. I search my memories of the last several hours, but it's all a little hazy.

Sergeant Guinsler is there; I remember he gave me the tour. We saw pictures of a tragedy on the television. And then he . . .

It comes back suddenly, all of it. Too much of it. I flinch as I remember the explosion, the fires, the bodies in offices, the people I saved. The baby. The collapse.

Looking for my dad!

I thought he was dead!

But he's here, holding me, and we're together!

I turn to him and give him the biggest hug any middle schooler has maybe given his dad in the history of middle schoolers. He's alive! He made it!

We're alive!

In my memory, I hear a dog barking.

I remember lying there in the dark, my thoughts jumbled, chewing gum. It was getting hard to breathe, hard even to think, though the gum helped. I heard the metal heap above me shifting. It had already fallen once and trapped me. I knew, as if by instinct, that it was going to fall again. I wouldn't survive when it did. I was going to die. I knew it, and somehow, I was okay with that. I was sad about it, sure, but I wasn't afraid. I didn't *want* it to happen but I couldn't change it, and I knew I'd helped people. I didn't regret a thing.

So I let go. I remember praying that my dad would be okay, and Sergeant Guinsler, and my mom. And I hoped, somehow, in some way, we'd all see each other again. I prayed that, in the meantime, they would all feel the love I felt for them, shining out like the warmth of a fire that cannot burn, like the safety of a roof that cannot fall. Like a memory that will never, ever fade.

And that was when I heard the barking.

Just at the moment I was drifting away from my body, that barking called me back. I'd thought it was a dream.

I lay there in that wreckage, laughing at my strange dream, but the barking didn't stop.

It was real.

It was faint at first, and then clearer, louder, sharper.

A real dog, barking at me.

I shouted back at it as loud as I could, "I'm here!"

The act of shouting made me cough and almost

choke on my gum. I spit it out, because yuck! I really didn't like cinnamon gum.

"I'm here!" I yelled again.

Soon, there was metal shifting, and wood moving, and light burst into my dark little place. I felt hands on me, arms pulling me. I was lifted out. Firefighters asked me my name, asked if I could hear them.

I answered as best I could, but there was a breathing mask on my face, so I just nodded and looked around at them.

"Chad?" I asked. Covered in their gear, they all looked like him, but none of them were.

"He's okay," they told me, and I smiled.

I didn't hear the dog barking anymore as the firefighters rushed me through the hallways so fast I could hardly tell where we were going. Hoses blasted all around us while more cleared the rubble from our path and called ahead for medics.

That's when I noticed the dog rushing along behind us—not barking, but holding a toy. Playing.

If this is still a dream, I thought, *it's a weird one*.

But it wasn't a dream. I'm here because that dog found me. I'm alive because these firefighters saved me. I'm with my dad, because he and Sergeant

Guinsler and all the people I helped today didn't give up on me.

"You were in there over an hour," my dad says to me through tears. He still hasn't let me go. "No one thought you could survive that long, but you did!"

"Told you he's a tough kid," Sergeant Guinsler says. He smiles at me. "You know you saved some lives today, Mikey?"

"Oorah," I grunt through my oxygen mask.

"Oorah," he says back.

"This is Sage," my dad tells me, pointing at the border collie in front of us. "He's the one who found you."

The dog perks up at the sound of his own name. I squint at him. I know his face. When the firefighters pulled me from the wrecked scaffolding, his face was the first I saw, barking up at me, tail wagging furiously.

"Do you want to meet him?" the handler asks me.

I stand slowly on wobbly legs. My left leg is bandaged pretty tight, and it hurts to put weight on it, but I balance myself with my dad's support. I hobble down from the ambulance bumper and pull the breathing mask off. I do my best to bend down and let the dog sniff my hand.

Sage's nose touches my scraped knuckles, then he shoves his head forward into my hand, letting me scratch his ears. He lets me run my fingers through the comfort of his soft fur, like he knows that's just what I need right now.

Then Sage flops over sideways and rolls onto his back for an epic belly rub.

"We've met," I tell the handler as I give Sage the belly rub of his life, his tail thumping the parking lot asphalt the whole time. "I'm really glad we did."

HISTORICAL NOTE

This is a work of historical fiction. The story is an invention, but it is based on the real events of September 11, 2001, at the Pentagon in Arlington, Virginia.

On the morning of September 11, 2001, groups of hijackers overtook airplanes on the East Coast of the United States and turned them into weapons. First, they crashed two passenger jets into the towers of the World Trade Center in New York City, then they crashed a hijacked airplane into the Pentagon. A fourth plane, which was being aimed back toward Washington, DC, did not make it to its target. The brave passengers on board tried to take back the plane from the hijackers and crashed in a field in Shanksville, Pennsylvania.

None of the airplane passengers survived any of these horrific crashes.

At the Pentagon that day, it was a normal morning of work for the headquarters of the United States Department of Defense, until 9:37 a.m., when five hijackers from Saudi Arabia crashed American Airlines Flight 77 into the western wall of E-Ring, killing themselves and all fifty-nine passengers and crew on board.

The airplane hit the first floor of the Pentagon while traveling about 530 miles per hour, spraying jet fuel and shrapnel all around. This led to unpredictable patterns of explosions and fire damage. The crash, the smoke, and the devastation that followed killed an additional 125 people on the ground and injured hundreds more.

The legacy of these terrorist attacks haunts us to this day, with impacts from how airport security works to decades of war in Afghanistan and Iraq.

Like a shock wave, the impacts of violence rippled out, shattering families and changing American society and politics forever. For a simple nonfiction introduction to the events of the day, readers eight years and older might want to check out *America Is Under Attack: September 11, 2001: The Day the Towers Fell* by Don Brown, an illustrated exploration of that day.

There are countless other stories and accounts written about that day, and this book is only meant as a fictional slice of a small part, a real-time story of what it might have been like inside the Pentagon. To write it, I drew on many nonfiction sources as well as my own knowledge and experience of the time, but it is, at heart, a work of fiction. To tell a compelling story, I had to make some changes from what really happened or could have happened.

In some cases, the characters are inspired by real people who were present on September 11, 2001, at the Pentagon, but the things the characters in this book do and say are my own inventions. There was no thirteen-year-old visiting his dad at work that day, though the office where Mikey's dad works is real. The Defense Intelligence Agency was gravely impacted by the crash, and the stories of those who survived are harrowing. Many in that office, sadly, were killed in the first seconds after impact.

There really was a woman with her baby in one of the offices near the crash site, and the baby really was blown out of its carrier. Thankfully, both the mother and the baby escaped with their lives.

Many others, however, were not so lucky. The general that Mikey and Sergeant Guinsler discuss in the early chapters was based on Lt. Gen. Timothy Maude, the highest-ranking military official to be killed in that attack. Additionally, the surgeon general of the Air Force that Mikey meets was based on the real officer, Lt. Gen. Paul K. Carlton Jr., who bravely helped lead rescue efforts in the crucial minutes after the attack that morning.

Those minutes were where I took the most liberties with changes to the story.

At one point, Sage the rescue dog thinks, *I start to wonder if I'll have anything to do, or if the people will have already all rescued each other before I get the chance.* This is, in fact, what happened. That morning was filled with amazing acts of heroism.

In reality, no one at the impact site would have survived for as long as Mikey and some of the others did. Anyone caught by the smoke and fire within the first half hour did not survive. Mikey's presence in that part of the building for over an hour is not realistic, though it is indicative of the heroism so many rescuers showed that day, rushing in to help others escape with their lives. And while there was no real "Mikey," there were countless soldiers, civilians, and firefighters who risked health and safety to bring others out alive.

For research, I relied heavily on a few sources: news

reports from the days, weeks, and months after the attack, and the PBS documentary *9/11 Inside the Pentagon*. I read several government reports, including the extremely detailed *Pentagon 9/11* from the Defense Studies Series, published by the Department of Defense Historical Office in 2007, and the book *Firefight: Inside the Battle to Save the Pentagon on 9/11* by Patrick Creed and Rick Newman, published by Ballantine Books in 2008.

As for Sage, there was a real dog named Sage whose regular handler really did get injured riding her horse, and the Pentagon really was his first mission. But he and his team were based out of New Mexico and flew in the day following the attacks. No rescue dog managed to find any survivors in the wreckage of 9/11, as no search and rescue dog was there in the minutes after the attack.

The real Sage did, however, discover many pieces of the airplane as well as the body of one of the hijackers, which was an important part of the investigation into who was responsible for this deadly incident.

As to what Sage could do, there has been a lot of research on how dogs make themselves understood by humans, how they make and adjust plans, and how they use their amazing sense of smell to perform lifesaving work in the aftermath of disasters.

I learned a lot from the American Rescue Dog Association's *Search and Rescue Dogs: Training the K-9 Hero*, 2nd edition, as well as Alexandra Horowitz's *Inside of a Dog: What Dogs See, Smell, and Know*. I also learned a lot from my own dog, Blueberry, a hound with an amazing nose and deep devotion to playing . . . though not to following my instructions.

For this book, I want to thank Orlando Dos Reis, whose concept for the story at Scholastic guided its creation, and Zachary Clark, my tireless editor, along with the amazing copy editor Bonnie Cutler and production editor Mary Kate Garmire, and the rest of the team at Scholastic, who work to get the right book to the right kid at the right time, with little fanfare but great dedication. Also, thanks, as ever, to my agent, Robert Guinsler, and a thanks to all the Department of Defense personnel who answered my questions in researching this book.

Lastly, I want to honor the real heroes and the far too numerous victims of this day in September 2001. I lived in New York City at the time and remember too well its horrors. The acts of terrorism that cut short so many lives cannot be forgotten, nor can the acts of bravery and kindness that followed. Tragedies too often are made by the deliberate cruelty of hateful ideologies, and often they spawn further cruelties from those who are hurting.

But those same tragedies can bring out the best in some of us. I hope we all learn to heed the call of healing and care that is possible even at our darkest hour, even at our most afraid and angry. Bravery and generosity are always a choice we can make, no matter the peril.

May the memories of those we lost on 9/11 and its aftermath around the world forever be a blessing and a warning that we must find a way to love each other, and to help whomever we are able, wherever we find them.

Alex London is the author of over twenty-five books for children, teens, and adults, with over two million copies sold. He's the author of the middle grade Battle Dragons, Dog Tags, Tides of War, Wild Ones, and Accidental Adventures series, as well as two titles in The 39 Clues. For young adults, he's the author of the acclaimed cyberpunk duology Proxy and the epic fantasy trilogy the Skybound Saga. A former journalist covering refugee camps and conflict zones, he can now be found somewhere in Philadelphia, where he lives with his husband and daughter, or online at calexanderlondon.com.